POLLY WANTS TO BE A
WRITER

Copyright © 2013 by Laura Michelle Thomas
First Edition – September 2013
Cover illustration by Ken Rolston

ISBN
978-1-4602-2819-7 (Paperback)
978-1-4602-2820-3 (eBook)

Produced by:

FriesenPress
Suite 300 – 852 Fort Street
Victoria, BC, Canada V8W 1H8

www.friesenpress.com

Distributed to the trade by The Ingram Book Company

EVERY GREAT WRITER STARTED OUT AS A WANNABE

POLLY WANTS TO BE A
WRITER

The Junior Authors Guide To
Writing And Getting Published

A Novel by
Laura Michelle Thomas

SO YOU WANNABE A WRITER

Do you recognize any of these thoughts?

> I can't think of anything to write. I'm
> too tired to write. I'll get to it later;
> there's too much going on right now.
> My ideas suck! The first draft has to
> be perfect. If I can just get the begin-
> ning right, the rest of the story will
> flow. I hate editing. It's good enough.
> I'll never figure out where to send
> my work. My parents want me to be a
> doctor, not a writer. I'll never make it
> as a writer. I might as well give up.

That's your literary dragon talking, your inner critic.
He is the Negative Nelly in your head who natters
at you and sends you writing in circles. He is the one
who stops you from finishing your first draft. If you do
finish, he is the one who whacks you upside the head
and tells you not to share your writing with the world
because you suck. Your dragon is an unruly perfection-
ist who tells you that nothing you write will ever be
good enough. Your dragon lies and lies and lies some
more. He is the reason wannabe writers, just like you,

get writer's block. Yes, he sounds awful, but he is also the key to your success as a writer. You just need to know how to use him.

Fortunately, as with most things in life, knowledge is empowering. That's what this book is about—empowering wannabe writers so they can become professional writers. Trust me, the world needs writers more than ever. Have you seen the Internet? From the local mom-and-pop flower shop to multinational farm equipment corporations, every business needs a good writer. From writing short stories for video games to writing press releases and blog articles, there are a ton of opportunities out there for aspiring young authors to write fiction or non-fiction for pay.

But, here is the thing, the truth about earning a living as a writer—to get there, to break through and get published and get paid—that offensive, distracting dragon inside you needs to be leashed and trained. Otherwise, you will be forever stuck with a computer full of good ideas and unfinished manuscripts.

So, how do you train your dragon and start to use him (or her) as an ally in achieving your writing dreams?

Every dragon is different, just like every writer is different, but there are tricks to the trade which I'm going to show you rather than tell you. By the time you get to the last page of the story, my three main characters—Polly, Ms. Whitford and Scrum—will have shown you how to get your inner, literary dragon under control so you can go from the idea stage to creating a solid, marketable piece of writing—in this case a short story—that can be confidently submitted to a publisher. By the time you finish reading this book, it is my hope you will have a better understanding of the publishing industry and what it takes to break into print and get your words into readers' hands.

To that end, getting your work out there for readers to enjoy, the afterword contains a short story writing challenge for you. You can skip to the end now and take a look, but I know you won't be able to do a good job unless you read Polly's story first and heed at least some of Ms. Whitford's advice. However, before letting you go on Polly's intriguing literary adventure, I would like to recognize the following individuals for their contribution to this novel and to my journey as a professional writer.

Artist and friend Ken Rolston, whom I believe is the "dragon master," did an amazing job bringing Scrum and Polly to life for the cover of the book. If you like his rendition of Scrum, then I suggest you stop by his website to marvel at the hundreds of "daily dragon drawings" he has done (www.KenRolston.com). I would also like to thank one of the junior copywriters at Laura Thomas Communications, sixteen-year-old Amneet Mann, for her topnotch proofreading of this manuscript. I would also like to thank my mother, Ricki Willing, for reading one of the earliest versions of this book and providing some truly valuable feedback on the story.

My daughter, Ella-Rose, has been my muse since she was born. While my beautiful nine-year-old insists that *Polly Wants to Be a Writer* is the best book she has ever read, I know she is patiently waiting for *The Adventures of Bob Warhop* to be finished. I promise, Ella-Rose, that I will get it done before Bob loses all his stuffing. (The main character of this children's fantasy novel is based on her stuffed ferret, Bob, so I'm sure you can appreciate her desire for me to get it done.) Likewise my husband, Alan Hewson, is begging me to finish *The Naked Storyteller*, a romantic comedy about a grade six teacher named Harry Tyke who has a midlife crisis after participating in a storytelling workshop. It's loosely based on my many years working as professional storyteller and leading workshops for teachers on professional days.

I must confess that without Alan's support, it would have been impossible for me to release *Polly Wants to Be a Writer* in 2013. I simply would not have had the time or strength to keep my own inner dragon in check without his constant encouragement and co-management of

Laura Michelle Thomas

our busy household. Being an avid fantasy reader, he also tore apart one of the early versions of this book and pointed out every inconsistency in the story. I am counting on him to continue to lift me up and critique my work as I get my next two novels ready for release in 2014. I know he will. Every writer needs an Alan. But you can't have mine.

Now, off you go. Have fun with Polly, and I look forward to hearing from you soon.

Keep writing,
Laura

CHAPTER ONE

Polly

Polly had a perfect idea for a story.

She stood in the compact bathroom of the two-bed-room apartment where she lived with her mom. Her dad, a globe-trotting tractor salesman, had lived there too, up until a month ago when her parents had decided they had given marriage enough of a try. Her dad had been mostly absent her whole life. Polly and her mom, a nurse, had enjoyed a relatively quiet life on their own in their little apartment for as long as she could remember.

The tip of the belt from Polly's pale pink bathrobe dangled just above the surface of the water in the toilet bowl as she hunched over to trim her toenails. She rested her bare right foot on the crescent-shaped, beige mat that wrapped around the base of the toilet. Her left foot was braced on the open rim of the toilet seat. She had her laptop open and running on the counter. Half of it hung over the edge of the sink. She had the record-ing program on, and while she snipped and smoothed her nails, she dictated her latest story idea.

This time, she assured herself, she would actually get it written—the whole thing from start to finish—and send it somewhere to be published. She knew this time she would really, one-hundred percent guaranteed, finish one of her own original stories. It would be fabulous, and the world would see what a great writer she truly was.

Ever since she had received a laptop from her school's One Laptop Per Child Program in grade six, Polly longed to be a writer. She wrote all the time and on everything. She kept a journal, of course. She wrote in school and on her computer, of course. But she also wrote on the inside of chocolate bar wrappers, and on the blank recipe cards her mom stored in the metal box beside the stove. Sometimes, when she was worried or stressed, she wrote on her arms, legs, hands, and feet. In fact, that morning when she was in the bathroom trimming her toenails and dictating her latest story idea (about a girl who found a silver bullet, which turned her into a creature that was half werewolf and half vampire, she had given it the species name "vamperwolf"), she had this poem written on her left foot:

> *The roast beast is black,*
> *Black as bruised midnight.*
> *Nighttime is here.*
> *This is all I can write.*

She had written the poem the previous evening while lying in bed. She had tried to put into words the new Sunday dinner ritual her parents had suddenly forced on her. It was part of her mom's campaign to show Polly "nothing has really changed." In some respects, her mom was right, things hadn't really changed. Her dad was still a smooth-talking tractor salesman who spent most of his time on the road—in far-away, fictional-sounding trade shows—slinging tractors and telling tall tales. But this new, Sunday family dinner ritual was unnerving for Polly. She couldn't remember any other time when she had had spent two unbroken hours sitting in the same room as her dad, not ever.

Polly's mom poked her head into the bathroom and frowned when she saw Polly's computer hanging over the edge of the sink. She was wearing her favourite pale pink nursing uniform.

Laura Michelle Thomas

"I'm going to the hospital for my shift now. Have a good day at school." She looked over Polly's shoulder and shook her head. "And, Polly, please stop writing on yourself, and my roast wasn't black. It was well-done because your father was late." When Polly didn't respond right away, she added, "Don't be upset at your father leaving. Everything will work out for the best, you'll see."

Polly said goodbye, but then, when she heard her mom open the front door to leave, she shouted that she would be home late because there was a special visitor coming to the library after school. Her mom shouted back that it was fine as long as she was home in time for dinner.

Polly waited to hear the heavy apartment door click shut. When it did, she sighed with relief. She really liked being home alone. It made her feel like writing. She took her foot off the toilet and looked at her reflection in the still water. It gave her an idea for a setting for her vamperwolf story, so she opened a blank document and typed a note for herself.

Polly's day was shaping up nicely. She had extra time to herself, she had some great notes for her vamperwolf story, and there was a visiting writer—a relative of Mr. Whitford, the high school principal—coming to the library after school. This writer, a Ms. Whitford, was looking for some teens to read and review her novel. There were only two spots available and, Polly had heard, she was going to pay the students for their time by giving them some one-on-one writing coaching.

Polly carried her laptop to her bedroom and set it up on her desk so it would be ready this evening when she wanted to write. She couldn't wait to get started on her vamperwolf story. Unlike all the other unfinished Polly originals on her laptop, this story was going to change everything. She was destined to have her work published. She just knew it.

Polly was on her fifth outfit by the time her friend, Natasha, knocked on the door. Polly had finally decided to go with the Bohemian look she believed was the hallmark of most authors: black leggings; a knee-length, swooshing floral skirt; short boots; and a baggy, open-knit purple sweater with a cream-coloured tank top underneath. She topped it off with a blue floral scarf, a white-knit tam over tousled hair, and a triple-spritz of her mom's perfume on her neck and wrists. The perfume was new. This was something she had never done before. But, Polly told herself, it was a special day, maybe a day that would kickstart her career. She was going to meet a published writer for the first time in her life.

When she opened the door, Polly was happy to see Natasha was also wearing black leggings, a floral skirt, an over-sized sweater, and a scarf. The main difference was that Natasha had finished the outfit with a thick braid and feather earrings, instead of copying Polly's loose hair and white tam.

As they walked to school, they talked about how they were going to get Ms. Whitford to choose both of them to read her book. Natasha suggested they bring their journals with them and look as if they had just finished a deep and profound writing session. Polly thought that would look too obvious. She told Natasha they should walk in carrying copies of the newest best sellers. It was, after all, a reading job. Natasha liked the idea. Then they tried to figure out where they should sit. Polly said the front row was out because it just wasn't cool, too desperate-looking. When Natasha suggested that keeners always sat in the front and maybe Ms. Whitford was looking for keeners, Polly shook her head and said the middle of the middle was the best place to be because you weren't in the back looking uninterested or in the front row looking desperate. Natasha agreed, and then she told Polly about a free short story contest for young writers she had found online. Polly said she had the perfect story in mind. It would definitely win a prize. She was sure of it.

★

Laura Michelle Thomas

The author visit did not go as planned.

Ms. Whitford—who turned out to be the opposite of Bohemian-looking with her hair pulled back into a bun, thick glasses, and a slate-grey business suit stretched over her plump frame—had not chosen Polly or Natasha to read her book. Polly was devastated. She believed that reading a book for an author would have led to her own fame and fortune as a writer. Polly envied the two students who had been chosen for no good reason Polly could understand. They were going to be invited to the book launch party and get to mingle with editors, publishers, and other writers; and they were each getting an hour of writing coaching with Ms. Whitford. They were going to get all that in exchange for being the first people to read her new novel which was about a girl and a dragon. All the other details about the book had been promptly chased out of Polly's mind by angry brain cells the moment she realized she had not been picked.

Polly sighed and leaned into her pillow. She looked over at her laptop. It was still on the desk where she had left it that morning. Polly thought about working on her vamperwolf story, but she just couldn't. She wasn't in the right head-space. She was tired and wouldn't be able to concentrate and do a good job. There was no point in even trying.

She sat forward, took a pen off her bedside table, and pulled her right foot close. She wrote:

> *The raw beast is white.*
> *White as pale midday.*
> *Daytime is there.*
> *That is all I can't write.*

"I can't do this!" Polly slammed her back against her pillow, causing the headboard to hit the wall. She grabbed a hardcover journal off her bedside table that had been sitting there, unused, since Christmas and threw it at the wall across the room.

Polly's room was quite narrow, so the fast-moving journal crashed forcefully into a small, antique mirror on the wall above her dresser.

A small circle of glass broke free of the mirror and fell onto her dresser. It reflected lamplight onto the ceiling in eery, round shimmers.

Polly got up and went over to examine the mirror. The white, wooden frame was thicker than the mirror itself, and the detail in the wood was intricate and swirly and reminded Polly of calligraphy. It was a baby shower gift from her grandma, her dad's mom, who had passed away before she could hold baby Polly in her arms. It had been hanging in Polly's room since before she was born.

Polly looked at herself in the mirror. There were no cracks or chips in the glass, just a perfectly round hole. Polly felt compelled to touch it, and when her fingers brushed the glass, she felt a sudden explosion of warm wet air on her fingertips.

Polly jerked her hand away. Goosebumps prickled her skin. It felt like someone, or something, had just sneezed on her. She sniffed the warm, sticky wetness on her fingertips. Sour and musty, the stink made her gag. Thinking she might throw up, Polly ran to the bathroom.

"Polly!" called her mom from the master bedroom. "It's late. Keep it down please and get yourself off to bed. School tomorrow."

"Okay, Mom."

Polly scrubbed her fingers with soap and sniffed them. The smell was still there. She gagged again.

Her mom called, "Are you sick to your stomach?"

Polly's forehead was clammy and her stomach felt queasy. She reacted similarly to airplane food and hospitals, only this was a few degrees worse. She doused a wash cloth with cold water, wrung it out, and held it to her forehead.

"Are you going to be sick? If you are, drink water, as much as you can, okay. That will help. Do you need me?"

"No. I'm okay, Mom. Goodnight."

Her mom appeared at the bathroom door. "Are you sure? You look pale."

"I'm okay. Just tired. I was working on a poem and just got a little excited."

Polly's mom looked down at Polly's bare feet. "I wish you would give up this writing-on-your-feet habit, but I'm glad you're okay. Wake me up if you need anything."

Polly smiled and nodded.

When her mom had gone back to bed, Polly searched the bathroom cupboards looking for the white cotton gloves her mom sometimes wore for overnight hand-softening treatments. She found them in a basket under the sink. She put a glove on the hand that had been sprayed, turned off the bathroom light, and went back to her room.

"Wake me up if you need me," called her mom.

"I will."

With her bedroom door firmly closed, Polly stood in front of the mirror, which was now hanging askew. Polly was sure that when she had left her bedroom, it had been hanging squarely on the wall. As she reached her gloved hand cautiously toward the hole again, she tried to imagine what had caused the explosion of foul wetness. Perhaps a sewer pipe had suddenly burst; that would be a rational explanation. But her writer's brain had other ideas. Polly wondered if she had found a portal to another world and now had alien snot on her fingers.

Polly held her gloved hand in front of the hole. Nothing happened. She stuck her index finger inside to see if she could provoke the same response. Nothing. Polly lifted the mirror off the wall, placed it face down on top of the round piece of glass on her dresser, and went to bed, keeping the one glove on her still-smelly hand.

That night, Polly dreamed about an albino dragon in a cave.

In her dream, the dragon dragged its snake-like, scrawny body over to a small round hole that was the only light source in its cave. It pressed its nostrils—two pink-rimmed circles, each one the size of a dinner plate—up against the hole and inhaled.

The dragon pulled the air in again, this time filling his lungs so deeply that, for a moment, its bony body looked like it had some meat on it. Then it belched loudly, turned around, and stuffed the spade-like flesh at the end of its tail into the hole like a cork.

The dragon belched again, holding the last note as long as it could. Then it stretched out its three-toed feet and scratched its pink claws into the cool dirt. It rolled its bony shoulders back, and opened and closed its wings twice, deliberately scraping its wing claws against the roof of the cave. Bits of rock and dust bounced off its scales. Then the dragon eased its long, pale body onto the dirt floor and exhaled loudly, scattering bits of wire, plastic, metal, and rock to the far corners of its cave. Then it closed its pink eyes and went to sleep.

In the morning, Polly woke up on the pink shag rug beside her bed. She could feel a tight, smooth coolness through the thin fabric of her pajamas. It was pressing on her entire body. Whatever it was, she could barely move. She wiggled and clawed and pushed against the bones and thin flesh that were wrapped around her.

"Who are you? Ouch!" it croaked.

Polly tried to scream, but the dragon—the albino dragon from her dream—had a tight grip on her chest and she could barely breathe.

Holding Polly securely with its tail, the dragon raised itself to its full height. It's horns grazed the ceiling making bits of paint and drywall rain down on both of them.

Polly struggled wildly and gasped for air.

The dragon unfolded its white, translucent wings. It brought its horned head down to where it could examine Polly's face. It had beady, pinkish eyes, black whiskers, and a white beard that touched the floor. It exhaled forcefully through its massive nostrils, causing Polly's hair to blow back off her face.

Polly gagged. It was the same stench she had been unable to wash off her fingers.

There was a soft knock on the door. "I'm leaving for work now, Polly. See you tonight."

The dragon was startled by the sound and let go of Polly.

She flopped to the floor, trying to catch her breath.

The dragon snarled at her, revealing sharp white teeth. Its whiskers twitched, and its eyes narrowed.

Instinctively, Polly punched the dragon between its grotesque nostrils, bolted out of her room, and shut the door. She stood panting in the hallway listening for sounds of the dragon coming after her.

From the entryway, Polly's mom called a final goodbye. Polly swallowed, took a breath, and returned the goodbye as calmly as she could. There was a dragon in her room, the albino dragon from her dream. Either that, or she was still asleep, stuck in her dream.

When the front door clicked shut, Polly turned around and faced her bedroom door. On the count of three, she opened it just wide enough to look inside. The dragon's smell hit her first. It wasn't a dream. There was an albino dragon curled up on her bed. Its head was tucked under its coils, but its tail was up and twitching.

Polly shut the door gently. There was only one person she could think of who might know what to do with a dragon.

CHAPTER TWO

Ms. Whitford

Polly was at Ms. Whitford's townhouse. She stared at the glossy green front door, her hand poised to lift the golden dragon door knocker. It had taken her a long time to find the address, and she was a tendril of raw nerves as she stood on the welcome mat worrying about what she was going to say and how she was going to say it.

Polly hugged her bike helmet and knocked. It was going to be warm day, and sweat was already breaking the pale surface of her skin. When no one answered, Polly stepped over to a window by the front door, pressed her nose to the glass, and peered inside. She could see a shadow, backlit, in what was probably the kitchen. Polly knocked again. This time, the shadow started walking toward the front door.

The door opened, and Ms. Whitford smiled. Her hair was in a bun as it had been the day before at the school. Her thick-rimmed glasses were perched on the end of her nose, and she wore a matronly, fuchsia blouse and black slacks. "I've been expecting you, Polly."

"Really?" stammered Polly. "How could you know I was coming?"

"I remember you from the library yesterday. I liked the white tam you were wearing. I haven't worn a hat like that for years. It looked so fashionable, I almost went out and bought one right after I left the school."

She waved Polly inside, but Polly's feet were rooted to the welcome mat. She was suddenly unsure about everything.

Ms. Whitford took Polly by both shoulders and pulled her through the doorway. "We can't have a decent conversation out here on my porch, can we? Let's have a cup of tea and get you to school before you find yourself in trouble."

Moments later, Polly's shoes were off and neatly tucked away in a shoe rack in the front hallway, and she was sitting on a slightly tattered denim-upholstered easy chair. Ms. Whitford's writing room, as she called it, was bright, airy, and lined with floor-to-ceiling bookshelves. There were two long windows in the far wall, across from where Polly sat, with a desk placed neatly between them. The desk held a tidy assortment of books; a jar filled with uniform HB pencils, all with their eraser ends up; an open notebook; a computer and printer; and a thick stack of printer paper that sat on top of an open leather folio. Polly thought the stack of paper might be Ms. Whitford's novel manuscript.

Ms. Whitford came back into the room carrying a tray full of tea things and a cinnamon bun. "I suspect you're upset a bit from what happened yesterday, and I like something sweet when I'm upset. Please have the cinnamon bun. I made them myself this morning."

Polly hesitated while the tea was poured. "How do you know so much about me?"

Ms. Whitford smiled and sat down in her desk chair. She blew on her tea to cool it as she studied the young girl in front of her. "I was just like you, once. The only thing I wanted in the whole world was to be a writer. I saw you sitting in the middle of the middle of the students trying to get my attention. It must have been quite a shock when I didn't select you as one of my readers. That's why you've come today. You want me to hire a third student to review my novel." She took a sip of her tea and then blew on it again.

Polly sighed. She didn't know whether or not she had come to the right place for help. Her problem had nothing to do with writing, or her craving to become a famous author; this was about the albino dragon in her bedroom. She stared at the manuscript on Ms. Whitford's desk, unsure of what she should say.

"Well? Are you here because you want to be my third reviewer and get your free hour of writing coaching and an invitation to the book launch party?"

Polly put her untouched tea back on the tray and stood up. "I'm sorry. This was a mistake. I'm late for school." She turned, ran out of the room and down the hallway to get her shoes.

Ms. Whitford came down the hall after her. "I have already called the school, Polly. They know you are here. I told them I am giving you a writing lesson. They expect you to be in class after lunch."

Polly held a shoe in one hand and stared at Ms. Whitford, who continued speaking as if knowing all these things about Polly was perfectly ordinary.

"I am happy to consider letting you join the other two in reading and critiquing my book. Come now and finish your tea, and we'll talk about your writing dreams. I want to get to know you before I turn you loose on my book." She took the shoes out of Polly's hands and smiled. "Okay? Come have tea with me."

Polly sagged with resignation, momentarily. Then, feeling a sudden flash of angry frustration, she lifted her eyes and looked directly through the lenses of Ms. Whitford's glasses. "I'm not here about writing or being your third reader. I'm here because you wrote a book about a dragon...and, whether you believe me or not, I woke up with a dragon in my bedroom this morning. It's big, ugly, an albino, and it stinks. I mean stinks. Smell my fingers!" Polly thrust her hand out in front of Ms. Whitford's nose.

Laura Michelle Thomas

Ms. Whitford smiled brightly. "It's always about a dragon, Polly. Come on down to my writing room and let's have our tea."

Polly was shocked by the fact that Ms. Whitford had not even blinked upon hearing she had a real, live, smelly dragon in her bedroom.

Back in the writing room with her cup of tea in her hands, Polly started to relax. She even thought she quite liked Ms. Whitford, who began asking Polly a series of questions which she said would help Polly learn to train her dragon.

"My dragon? It's not mine, and I don't want to train it!" protested Polly. "I need it gone for good, or my mom is going to go ballistic. Our landlord doesn't even allow goldfish unless you fill out a ten-page application form."

"I need you to focus, please. This is nothing to get hysterical about. I am just going to ask you some questions about your dragon."

"It's not my dragon...well, maybe it is...but if we get evicted..." Polly sighed.

"That won't happen. I promise." Ms. Whitford picked up one of her perfectly sharpened pencils and took a small, spiral-bound notebook out of her desk drawer. "Now, I need to get to know this wonderful creature in your bedroom. First question: How do you think the dragon got into your room?"

Polly thought about it for a minute, then answered, "I think through a hole in an antique mirror that's been in my room since before I was born."

Ms. Whitford made a note in her notebook. "How did your mirror come to have a hole in it, or has it always had a hole?"

Polly was embarrassed. "I was mad. I threw my journal...it hit the mirror and broke off a perfectly round piece of glass."

Ms. Whitford didn't look up from her notes, but kept writing as she asked, "What were you mad about?"

"Stuff."

"Hmm...did any smells or other sensations come out of the hole in the mirror?"

"Yes."

"Can you describe them, please, in detail?"

Polly held up her hand. "Something sneezed on my fingers when I put them up to the hole. It was wet, a spray, and the smell made me feel sick."

"What did it smell like?"

"Bad. I don't know how to describe it better than that."

"Try to find the words."

"I can't. I don't know the right words."

Ms. Whitford opened a drawer and took out a sheet of paper. She held it out to Polly.

Polly waved it away. In her imagination, she could see the dragon's pasty, white body; but she couldn't think of the right words to describe its smell. She stood up. "I have to go and—"

"No, you don't, Polly. Sit down and listen. I am going to tell you something that will help you focus on what we are doing right here, right now, in this room. Do you understand?" Ms. Whitford shook the piece of paper at her.

Polly nodded and took the paper. It had adjectives on it, broken into five lists by sense, including a list of adjectives used to describe a wide variety of smells.

Ms. Whitford sat back in her desk chair. "I need your whole mind and imagination to be here with me right now, okay? I know dragons, and I can help you with yours. I promise."

Polly looked at the list. "Are you sure?"

"One hundred percent satisfaction guaranteed."

Polly examined the woman's face for signs of doubt. There were none.

"Look at the list and choose the word that best describes your dragon's smell."

Polly looked at the list, chewing her lower lip. This was one of the things she didn't like about words. Finding the perfect word to describe something was really hard. When she was writing and got stuck like this, she would usually slam her laptop shut and write on herself.

Ms. Whitford waited. "Just pick one of the words, one you know the meaning of."

Polly scanned the list looking for a word she recognized: acidy, acrid, aromatic, balmy, briny, burnt, damp, dank, etc. There were at least thirty words on the list, but she couldn't think of the right one to describe the dragon's smell. She thrust the paper back at Ms. Whitford. "Bad. The smell was bad, and that's all I can think of right now."

Ms. Whitford put the paper away and wrote in her notebook. She looked at Polly. "How do you feel about working with me on your writing every day?"

"Writing? No, thank you. I need help with the dragon in my bedroom. I thought you could help me with it, not my writing."

"You need help with your writing, plain and simple." Ms. Whitford sipped her tea.

"No. I need help getting that dragon out of my apartment."

Ms. Whitford leaned forward in her chair and held her tea cup with both hands. "You want to be a writer. Am I correct?"

Polly looked at Ms. Whitford and admitted, "Really badly since grade six."

Ms. Whitford rubbed her chin thoughtfully and hesitated before she spoke. "Polly...you are not going to like what I have to say, but there is no getting rid of that dragon, not safely. He, or she, is here to stay. Your only hope is to train him or her, and you must stop referring to your dragon as an it. I won't have that kind of disrespect in my home." Ms. Whitford stood up and put a hand on the manuscript on her desk. She looked at Polly. "I will teach you how to train your dragon."

Polly looked up at Ms. Whitford, her eyes were wide. "Can't it—I mean the dragon—just go back to where it came from?"

"What? Through the mirror? No, Polly. Once a dragon pops out, there's no going back. The mirror is still a doorway of sorts, but it won't take you anywhere you want to be."

"Does the dragon know that?" asked Polly.

"He or she might, but, then again, possibly not. It depends on—anyway, Polly, it was nice meeting you. That's it for today. I can begin working with you tomorrow after school."

"But, the dragon, what do I do with it—I mean him or her—until then?"

"For starters," Ms. Whitford smiled, "find out your dragon's name and what he or she likes to eat. Then give your dragon something to eat. That's your homework."

"But I don't want a dragon."

"Oh, don't say that, Polly. You don't realize yet how lucky you are to have one. And, the thing is, you two are already bonded for life. But the bond is immature. You need to get to know your dragon and vice versa. The more you trust each other, the stronger your bond—and your writing—will be."

Polly politely thanked her, said goodbye, and was soon in Ms. Whitford's driveway, straddling her bike and doing up her helmet clasp. She stepped on the pedal and coasted down the driveway.

"I forgot to tell you something!" shouted Ms. Whitford, running out.

Polly hit the brakes and turned around.

Ms. Whitford took hold of Polly's handlebars. "Never tell your dragon, out loud, that you wish he or she was dead. Never utter anything like that to your dragon. Do you understand? Promise me."

Polly didn't say anything, but she was thinking it would be nice to have her bedroom back and not have to worry about upsetting her mom.

Ms. Whitford pushed her glasses back up the bridge of her nose and looked directly into Polly's eyes. "Just promise me you won't speak like that to your dragon. If you do, you will never be a writer."

"What if it tries to hurt me?" asked Polly.

"Trust me." Ms. Whitford smiled. "Dragons like this one are not prone to violence. He or she is just as scared and confused as you are."

★

Polly rushed home after school that day with a mixture of excitement and fear. Ms. Whitford had been so calm, as if coming face to face with a dragon was as ordinary as homework. Her task, which to Polly seemed absolutely impossible, was to find out the dragon's name, what it eats, and then get it some food.

Trembling, Polly put her hand on the doorknob and braced herself. Her only comfort was knowing the dragon was, possibly, just as scared and confused as she was. She really hoped it was true.

Polly decided to knock first.

There was no answer.

Polly opened the door just wide enough to look inside. Her room still stunk, and the albino dragon was still there, curled up on her bed with its pointed tail draped over the side and hanging just above the floor. The tip twitched back and forth.

Polly stepped into the room and closed the door behind her. She kept a hand on the doorknob just in case she needed to make a quick exit.

The dragon raised its ugly head and snorted. Its long snake-like scales rippled with tension. Polly had a strange feeling the dragon was a he.

Polly stayed as far away from him as she could. "What's your name?" she said quickly.

The dragon bristled and narrowed his pink eyes. He snorted, louder this time.

"It's okay. I'm your friend. What's your name?"

The dragon began to slither off the bed and move toward Polly. "It's you!" His voice was low, and it wavered slightly.

"What do you mean it's me?"

"Your voice. I know your voice. I heard it in my cave. You say terrible words about roast beef. It's you!" The dragon's voice grew calmer and firmer as he spoke.

Polly felt like she had been punched in the gut. "How do you—"

"This is my home!" The dragon belched rudely, interrupting himself. "You and your words should go away."

Polly bristled and lowered her tone. "You are stinking up my room. You should leave."

The dragon walked on short legs toward Polly. His tail was as stiff as a board and twitching aggressively. "It's mine."

When he was just a few steps away, Polly heard a rumbling sound. "Would...would you like something to eat?" she asked.

The dragon stopped where he was. His eyes widened. His long stomach growled again as he nodded.

Polly took her hand off the doorknob and asked, "What do you eat?"

The dragon pursed his pink lips and furrowed his bony brow. "I don't know what they are called, but I found one over there, and I ate it. It was delicious."

"What? Where?" Polly had no idea what thing of hers he might have eaten.

The dragon pointed his nose at Polly's desk. Polly looked. It took her a moment to realize what had happened. The dragon had eaten her laptop. Every story idea she had written down since grade six was gone.

"You eat laptops?" she snapped at him, her fear gone. "Bad dragon!"

"Laptops good." He narrowed his eyes and growled at Polly. "I want more."

"Only if you tell me your name."

"Bring me laptops!"

"Fine!" Polly stomped her foot and clenched her fists like she was five years old again. "Stay here. I'll be right back."

Laura Michelle Thomas

She glared at the dragon as she opened the door and stormed out of her bedroom.

She went to the family change jar in her mom's closet and counted out twenty dollars. There was only one place she was going to be able to find cheap laptops, and she needed to get there and back before her mom got home from her shift at the hospital.

CHAPTER THREE

Scrum

Polly was in the lobby of her apartment building waiting for the elevator. She had two large bags from the recycling depot draped over the top tube of her bike and needed to beat her mom upstairs.

After striking the deal with the dragon, Polly had ridden her bike to the local recycling depot, where she wasted nearly an hour haggling with a chubby, pimply-faced clerk. After negotiating him down from fifty dollars to twenty dollars, Polly came away with five ancient laptops. She still felt ripped off, especially knowing the parts were going to end up in the dragon's skinny guts. But she hoped it would work, and that she would learn the dragon's name. When the clerk had given her a funny look, Polly told him she was going to build a new laptop out of the parts. He had chuckled and teased her about being the prettiest computer nerd he had ever seen. Then he had watched her count out twenty dollars in loose change with a weird smirk on his face.

Polly was too late. Her mom had just come out of the underground parking garage and was approaching the glass doors of the building. She waved at Polly and motioned for her to unlock the latch and let her in.

The elevator door opened. Polly waved at her mom and rolled her bike inside. Polly's mom looked surprised and then annoyed. She unlocked the front door of the building just in time for Polly to hear her name being called in an angry tone.

Polly pushed the button for her floor repeatedly, trying to hurry the elevator along. Her mom would take the stairs and probably be standing there when the doors opened with her hands on her hips and a frown on her face.

The elevator stopped with a bounce at Polly's floor.

Polly tried to think of a logical reason why she would have bags of laptops hanging off her bike. The doors opened. The hall was empty, but Polly could hear her mom's voice coming from the stairwell. She was walking up with a neighbour.

Polly blitzed down the hallway and got herself, her bike, and the laptops put away as quickly as she could.

When her mom walked into the apartment, Polly was in the kitchen tearing lettuce into a salad spinner. "Sorry, Mom. I had to go to the bathroom really badly. I couldn't wait."

"Yes. I can smell that. Use the fan next time, please."

Polly sniffed. The apartment did smell...bad.

Polly's mom washed her hands, took some chicken out of the fridge, and started to pound it flat with a meat tenderizer. They worked quietly, side by side, until Polly's mom stopped pounding and looked at Polly. "Open a window, please. The apartment reeks. One of the neighbours must have left their compost bucket in the hallway again."

Polly went through the living room and opened the sliding glass door to the balcony. It smelled significantly fresher and cleaner outside than it did in the apartment. How long, she wondered, could she keep a bad-smelling dragon a secret?

Polly walked to the railing and looked along the side of the building to see if she could see into her bedroom window. She couldn't because of the reflection on the glass at that angle, but she noticed the building across the way had a clear view inside her room. What if they saw the dragon through her bedroom window and called the police?

Polly went back to the kitchen.

Her mom was breading the flattened chicken. "We have company coming over after dinner tonight. I met an interesting woman while I was on my lunch break at the hospital. It turns out she knows your father. I tried to get ahold of your dad, but he never answers his phone."

Polly groaned at the thought of another awkward visit. "I'm not very hungry. I'm going to my room."

"Do you have any homework tonight?"

"Always."

"What's the matter with you?" said her mom, wiping her hands on a tea towel.

"My laptop...I...I dropped it...it's wrecked." Polly felt tears sting her eyes as it sunk in that every story idea she had ever come up with was churning away in the skinny dragon's digestive juices.

"Is that why you had those bags hanging off your bike when you came home? Did you borrow a computer from one of your friends at school?"

"Sort of." Polly didn't know what else to say. Somehow, she just couldn't bring herself to tell her mom about the dragon.

Polly's mom gave her a hug. "I'm so sorry to hear about your laptop. Are you sure it's completely wrecked?"

Polly nodded.

"Maybe we can get it repaired, and you can use my new one in the meantime."

"Thanks, Mom. I'm going to my room until dinner. Homework."

"Okay, Polly, and cheer up. A broken laptop isn't the end of the world."

Polly shrugged and walked out of the kitchen.

She went to the closet where she had stashed the laptops and pulled out the heavy bags. She went to her bedroom, opened the door, and stepped quietly inside.

Laura Michelle Thomas

She hardly recognized it; everything she had was gone, destroyed, decimated, ruined.

Her bedroom was dim, almost completely dark. The dragon had shattered and smashed and shredded every piece of furniture, every piece of clothing, every book, blanket, picture, and knickknack. He had piled up most of the debris in front of the bedroom window. Polly imagined the rubble must look suspicious from the neighbour's point of view.

Polly clutched the bags of laptops. The dragon was curled up tightly in the corner of the room where her bed used to be. She could only see him in the gloom because of his glowing, colourless skin.

Polly turned on the bedroom light to take a closer look at the wreckage.

The dragon picked up his ugly head and sniffed the air.

"I brought you these for dinner." Polly opened a bag and took out one of the laptops. "But you have to tell me your name first."

Without hesitation, the dragon told her his name. "Scrum."

"Scrum?"

"Scrum," said Scrum.

Polly dropped both bags of laptops on the floor. "I hope you choke on these."

Furious, she left the room, slamming the door behind her. She stood in the hallway fuming. A touch on her shoulder startled her.

"Since when do we slam doors in this house?" Polly's mom was holding her new laptop. "Let's go set this up on your desk."

Polly's mom went to open the door to Polly's room.

Polly grabbed her hand to stop her from opening the door. "Mom. No."

Her mom frowned. "What's going on?"

"My room is a mess. I'm kind of embarrassed."

Her mom pushed past her and opened the door.

Polly braced herself. She had left the light on. Scrum stood in the middle of the room swallowing the last of the five laptops, the corners and edges making ugly bulges in his scaly flesh.

The room stank.

Scrum belched loudly. Then he noticed the new laptop and smiled. "Lovely! You brought me dessert!" he said, salivating. His pink eyes were fixed on Polly's mom who was walking across the room to the far wall where Polly's desk used to be.

Polly waited for the yelling to start. But it didn't.

Polly's mom said nothing about Scrum. It was as if she did not see him or the mess.

Scrum unfurled his wings, reached his head toward Polly's mom, and sniffed the laptop. "Delicious," he said, opening his mouth. Drool dripped from his lower jaw, trickled down his beard, and oozed onto the carpet.

"No!" shouted Polly, grabbing the laptop out of her mom's hands.

"Polly! What's wrong with you?"

Polly looked at her mom with wide eyes. "Don't you see him?"

"Who? Oh! My goodness, it smells putrid in here! We need to do a spring cleaning this weekend. Did you bring home a pet or something?"

"No, Mom. Can't you see him?" Polly nodded in Scrum's direction.

"Who?"

"The albino dragon. He's standing right in front of you. He wants to eat your new laptop for dessert."

Polly's mom looked in the direction Polly was indi-cating. She grimaced. "Let me feel your forehead." She put her palm on Polly's forehead. Scrum just stood and watched. "Warm...hmm...you'll feel better once you have something in your stomach."

Polly followed her mom, and the laptop, out of her room and closed the door behind her.

When dinner was finished, Polly helped her mom wash the dishes. Her mom was unusually quiet and kept glancing at Polly with a serious expression as she clanged around the kitchen putting plates and pots away. Polly tried to play the part of a sick, but not crazy, daughter. She had a bad feeling about her mom's thoughts. Mental illness ran in her mom's family. Polly's aunt suffered from bipolar disorder and had just checked herself in to a private depression clinic. Polly worried her mom was thinking she was having some kind of emotional breakdown, so she coughed and sniffed and acted like she was just really tired or coming down with a cold. Maybe her mom would forget Polly's comments about the dragon in her room, but she doubted it. There were going to be phone calls to the extended family for sure.

The doorbell rang.

It was the guest her mom had talked about earlier, a friend of her dad, a Dr. Miriam Mammozarack. She introduced herself as an inventor and a counsellor. Though she was about the same age as her parents, she looked old and severe. Her face was sharp, her hair was oily and pulled back into a thin greasy ponytail that sat limply on one shoulder.

Moments after entering the apartment, the doctor said the air was rancid and requested the windows be opened to let the putrid air out. Then she curtly asked Polly's mom to send Polly to her room, which she did.

Polly went to her room, glad to have been excused.

Scrum blinked his pink eyes at her from the pile of debris by the bedroom window. Polly sat down in the shredded mess that used to be her bed, found a pen in the wreckage, and wrote on the back of her hand:

> *Dumb Scrum is Glum.*
> *Glum Scrum is Dumb.*
> *Dumb-glum is Scrum.*

Scrum shifted his bulk and a still-intact cover of *Charlotte's Web* slid down the pile and landed on the floor.

"I'm not dumb or glum," he said with snort. Then he pulled his head into the debris pile and disappeared.

CHAPTER FOUR

Pencils

Polly was alone in Ms. Whitford's writing room, waiting for her to come back with tea. To pass the time, she paced around the room, running her fingertips along the rows of book spines. Every time she passed by Ms. Whitford's desk, she couldn't help but notice the manuscript, which was now wrapped in the leather folio and secured with long leather laces tied in a neat bow. Polly thought back to Ms. Whitford's school visit. She couldn't remember what the title was, just that the story had something to do with dragons. Polly fingered the leather laces and then, without realizing it, started to pull the bow loose.

"Here we are," said Ms. Whitford, coming in with the tea tray. She plunked it down on the low table between her desk chair and the denim-upholstered easy chair. "Tell me what you think a writer is, Polly."

Polly had bolted to the easy chair as soon as Ms. Whitford had come in. She smoothed her skirt and cleared her throat. "A writer is someone who works for a publishing company and gets all their stories published."

Ms. Whitford, who had been leaning forward pouring tea, laughed out loud. "Ha! Okay. Let's start at the beginning." She handed Polly a blank sheet of paper on a clipboard. "We're going to do a warm up exercise. I am going to time you for sixty seconds. You are going to use this slippery pen to write fast and without stopping."

"I can't write...I'm not...I'm uncomfortable." Polly preferred to write alone on her laptop in her bedroom, not in front of a stranger in a strange place on a clipboard.

Ms. Whitford narrowed her eyes. "And your bedroom, how comfortable is it right now?"

Polly accepted the pen and the clipboard. She looked at the paper. There were no lines on it, which really bothered her. "What do I write about?"

"Whatever comes out of you. I want you to write, not think."

"But I have to think."

"No, you can just write."

"But I—"

"Don't think. Write fast. Don't worry about mistakes. Just write. I don't want your pen to stop, not even for a split second. Ready. Set. Go!" She flipped over a miniature hour-glass-shaped timer filled with white sand.

Polly held up the clipboard. "I can't write on this thing."

Ms. Whitford looked at Polly and raised an eyebrow. "You can have my desk."

They traded places, but it didn't help. Polly didn't understand what Ms. Whitford wanted or how this was going to help train Scrum. She glanced at Ms. Whitford and asked, "Will we be done early enough for me to go to the recycling depot? I need more laptops for Scrum."

Ms. Whitford smiled. "Scrum. Interesting name. It's commonly associated with confusion and a great deal of kicking and screaming, if you're a rugby fan. Would you like to know how to introduce Scrum to some new foods, to something a little easier and cheaper than laptops?"

"Oh, yes! Of course!"

Ms. Whitford smiled. "Then do this quick writing exercise, and I will tell you the secret."

"Okay," Polly agreed. "I'm ready."

"Right!" Ms. Whitford picked up her timer. "Don't think. Don't stop. Just write. Let the words spill out of you quickly with no internal editing. Ready. Set. Go!"

Ms. Whitford had been right about the pen being slippery. Polly's first letter shot like a bullet across the blank page leaving an indigo trail behind it. "Can I start again? I messed up."

Ms. Whitford put a hand to her forehead and sighed. "No. Just write, Polly. I can't make it any clearer."

Polly looked at the ruined paper. She just couldn't do it. Not here in this room, not without thinking. She couldn't turn off the voice in her head that was saying she needed to have a topic before she could write.

Ms. Whitford went over to her bookcase and took down a squat, bulbous vessel painted bright gold. She held it up and asked, "What is this?"

"A flower vase?"

"Not quite. It's an urn. Inside this urn is...well...it's an urn. Let's just leave it at that, for now. Was this always an urn?"

"I'm not sure. I think so."

"No. Think about it, Polly. What was it before it took this shape?"

Polly thought for a moment and then guessed. "Clay?"

"Exactly right!" Ms. Whitford smiled and put the golden urn on her desk. She picked up a pencil. "What is this?"

Polly rolled her eyes. "A pencil."

"Good girl!" Ms. Whitford's smile widened. "There is hope for you yet!" She put the pencil down next to the urn. "Which of these objects would you like to feed your dragon? Either one is more convenient than laptops. Your choice."

Polly pointed to the pencil.

"Good choice. Dragons like Scrum prefer to eat writing instruments. So, let's try the exercise one more time. Then, I will tell you how to add pencils to Scrum's

Laura Michelle Thomas

diet." She put a fresh sheet of unlined paper in front of Polly.

Polly picked up the slippery-ink pen. "I'm ready."

Ms. Whitford nodded. "Sixty seconds. Write fast. Don't think. Keep your hand moving. Ready. Set. Go!" She flipped over the timer and let the sand run.

This time, Polly was able to do the exercise but not entirely without thinking. The critical, worrywart voice in her head kept breaking the spell and slowed the movement of her hand across the page. It choked the flow of words by insisting she think first and write second. When the sand ran out and Ms. Whitford told her to stop writing, Polly looked down at the paper. She had only written one sentence: *I hope I can get Scrum to eat pencils instead of laptops.* The sentence lay in a perfect, horizontal line across the page. There wasn't a single spelling mistake. Polly felt as if she had done an excellent job.

"Mind if I take a look?" said Ms. Whitford.

Polly handed her the paper.

Ms. Whitford frowned. "This won't do at all." She flipped over the sheet of paper. "You need to try again. Let go. Let yourself make mistakes. This is no time to be perfect. Ready. Set—"

"I'm not ready!"

"Go!" Ms. Whitford turned over the timer.

This time Polly pushed her pen into the paper and let her emotions scream across the page in random gibberish. She wrote hotter and faster than she had ever written in her life, and when the white sand ran out, she had sweat on her brow, goosebumps on her skin, and an electric shiver running through her spine. Her jaw was clenched, and her eyes stung. Looking down at the inky scrawl, she felt free and strangely powerful. She looked up at Ms. Whitford, knowing she had done well.

"Well done. You will do this same write-without-thinking exercise for two minutes tomorrow."

★

Polly sat cross-legged on her bedroom floor in front of the debris pile, which Scrum seemed to have claimed as his permanent nest. She could hear the dragon's stomach rumble with hunger, but she couldn't get him to even sniff the attractively-arranged plate of pencils she had set out for him. She presented the pencils in an enticing way, just as Ms. Whitford had instructed. Just like a child who wants candy for dinner, Ms. Whitford had told her, the dragon would eat them when he was good and hungry. But, so far, it had not worked. Scrum would not touch the pencils.

Polly picked up a single pencil and twisted it anxiously in her hands, trying to figure out what to do next. She twisted so hard the eraser came off in her hand.

Polly's mom came into the room. She held out her laptop. "I thought you might need this for your homework tonight."

Polly dropped the pencil, and its detached eraser, as she sprung up to intercept her mom. "I'll work on it in the kitchen, Mom. Thanks." Polly grabbed the laptop out of her mom's hands, closed her bedroom door, and went to the kitchen.

Her mom followed. "What happened to your grandmother's mirror? It's not hanging on the wall anymore."

Polly was surprised. Ms. Whitford had told her that her mom could not see any of the damage Scrum had done to her room. "I...ah...it fell."

"Well, you should hang it up again. It's a special piece of your past. I never told you this before, but your grandmother was a poet, not published, but she wrote all the time, apparently. Your dad told me that the first time we discussed your habit of writing on yourself."

"Um, okay. I'll hang it back up later." Polly sat down at the kitchen table and turned on the laptop.

Her mom came over and gave her a hug from behind. "You won't be going to school right away tomorrow morning. I've made an appointment for you with Dr. Mammozarack. I need you to ride your bike over to her office and then go straight to school after you talk to her, okay? I'll come next time. Goodness, Polly! What's on your hand? Scrum? Dumb? I wish you would stop doing this to yourself. It's not good for your skin. What's wrong with all those journals I've bought you?"

Polly closed the laptop. "I'm going to bed."

"This early?"

Polly shrugged and stood up. "I'm tired. It's been a long day."

"I know. Your dad has been moved out for a month now. I'm sure Dr. Mammozarack will be able to help. She specializes in working with teenage girls who are going through a rough patch."

There it was. Polly's mom thought she was going crazy. Who ever heard of an inventor-counsellor anyway? Polly hadn't. It sounded weird, but there was nothing Polly could do about it now except act as normal as possible.

Polly said goodnight to her mom, went to her room, and closed the door. It smelled awful, and she wondered why Scrum smelled so bad.

She turned on the lights.

The plate of pencils had been turned over, and they were all missing their erasers. There were no teeth marks. The metal tubes that held the erasers were simply empty.

Scrum's stomach gurgled loudly from under the pile of debris.

"Do you want to try the rest of the pencils now? They're delicious. See. Even better than the erasers." Polly stuck one between her teeth and pretended to gnaw on it. "Yummy in my tummy."

"Gimmee!" Scrum lunged and grabbed the pencil Polly had in her mouth with his teeth. The sudden movement and the wetness against her face made her shriek.

In a split second, her mom was standing in the doorway. "Why are all those pencils on the floor?"

"I thought I saw a mouse. But I didn't," Polly laughed, trying to sound normal and not like she had just been slimed by a dragon. "Sorry." She picked up the pencils.

"Please open your window and let some fresh air in here before you do anything else."

Polly could see the strain on her mom's face as she turned and closed the bedroom door.

The instant the door clicked shut, Scrum scrambled out of his nest. The rubble exploded around him as he came at Polly. Polly backed away from him, her instincts telling her to be afraid. She had a dragon in her bedroom, a big, hungry one, who was even uglier than he smelled. Polly inched backwards holding the pencils in front of her like a miniature sword.

Scrum bent down, and with a single swipe of his jaws, clamped down on all the pencils Polly was holding. She let go. The dragon tipped his head back and swallowed. Polly could see the pencils sliding in a mass down his narrow, white throat.

Scrum belched. "I'm still hungry."

Polly had backed herself into the wall where her desk used to be. "I have another package in my school bag." She pointed at the canvas bag, which she had left by the bedroom door.

Scrum nodded his approval, and Polly realized she had to do something to teach the dragon that she was in charge, not him. She went to her bag and opened it. There were five more packages of HB No. 2 pencils at the bottom. She took out one.

Polly deepened her voice and spoke firmly. "Okay, Scrum. I have a treat for you." She faced him, held out the pencil, and waved the eraser in front of his cavernous nostrils.

Scrum inhaled deeply and opened his mouth. Saliva pooled and began to dribble.

Polly shook her head and put the pencil behind her back. "Not until you sit."

"Sit?" He seemed genuinely confused. "Why would I do that?

Laura Michelle Thomas

"Because I said so, and I am the boss here. This is my room, my rules, and I said sit!"

The dragon opened his scrawny wings and pulled himself up to his full height. He seemed to fill the entire bedroom with his pale, bony body. Polly could see a flame-coloured glow pulsing under the white scales of his belly. He opened his mouth and belched an acrid cloud of smoke into the room.

Polly gagged. She wrapped her arms around her face. "Please! I'll do anything you want. Just don't burn me."

"Anything?" He exhaled another cloud into the room. It wafted over and gathered around Polly's head and shoulders.

"Anything. Just don't burn me."

"There are three things you must do for me."

"Anything." Polly looked down at the floor to avoid his gaze.

"Good." Scrum sat down on the floor in front of Polly like an obedient dog. "First, you must bring me laptops to eat every day, maybe with some pencils on the side, but not too many."

Polly nodded.

"I can't hear you."

"Okay!"

"Second," the dragon continued with a more serious tone, "you must never enter my room unless you have food for me."

Polly nodded, but did not reply.

Scrum snarled and narrowed his eyes until they were just pink slits. The ridge of his brow protruded like the brim of a baseball hat. "Look at me. Look at me and obey."

Polly kept her eyes on the floor. She was tired of this. She wanted her life back. She wanted her room back. She wished the dragon would just go away forever.

The dragon growled again. "I said—"

Polly snapped her head up and met Scrum's pink gaze. The forbidden words spewed out of her mouth: "I wish you were..." Polly stopped herself. She did not know what would happen to the dragon if she finished the sentence. Maybe the fire inside him would ignite or explode, killing them both.

"You wish I was what?" Scrum blinked his eyes at her. He looked like a grotesque, white puppy.

"Never mind." Polly took a deep breath and exhaled. "I'll get you laptops. I promise." She sat down next to him, still holding the pencil.

"Can I have that?"

Polly opened her hand and let him eat it.

Laura Michelle Thomas

CHAPTER FIVE

Training

"You're not supposed to say anything like that to your dragon. Never!" said Ms. Whitford. Her face was red and blotchy.

Polly sat at Ms. Whitford's desk. She had just finished her write-without-thinking exercise. In two minutes she had written three messy lines, which Ms. Whitford had praised her for. Then she had asked for an update on Scrum. When Polly told her what she had almost said, Ms. Whitford knelt down in front of Polly, put a hand on each of her shoulders, and said, "Do you understand what will happen if you say those words to Scrum and mean them?"

Polly wiggled her shoulders free. "He will die or explode or something?"

"Yes. He will die. He will turn into a cold pile of white ashes, and do you know what else will happen?"

Polly shrugged.

"You won't ever be a writer."

Polly shrugged again. "I don't care."

"Why would you say that?"

"I suck. I'll never make it. I get writer's block every ten seconds, every day, all the time. I should give up. I can't even finish any of my own stories. I truly suck. I'm sorry for wasting your time. Maybe I'll be a nurse like my mom or sell farm equipment like my dad. Whatever! I'm going to go home and tell Scrum I wish he was dead and get on with my life."

Ms. Whitford got up off her knees and looked out the window. "The fact that you have Scrum is proof you have some of what it takes to be a writer. When it comes to writing, you and Scrum are one. He is your ticket to making it in this profession. You can make it, but you have to train him."

"I don't understand. You mean Scrum is me?"

"Yes and no. If you die, he dies. He cannot live without you. But if he dies—because you kill him with your words—you will still live, but not as a working writer. You will be haunted by ideas and a deep longing to write, but that thing that makes writers different from ordinary people—the ability to take an idea and turn it into a highly readable piece of writing—will be gone. You will never become an author of any kind without Scrum. Living without Scrum would be like living with a phantom limb, but the pain would never really go away."

Polly's arms prickled with goosebumps. It was sinking in. In nearly killing Scrum, she had nearly killed her only chance at becoming a writer. She looked up at Ms. Whitford, who was still staring out the window into her garden. A light rain was falling.

She turned to face Polly. "Your challenge then, just as it has been ever since writer-types began telling stories around campfires, is to train your dragon. You have to use him to become the writer you are destined to be. Honestly, he is going to require every ounce of discipline, patience, and love you have in those bones of yours. If you don't train him, he will become nothing more than a laptop-eating nuisance who continually destroys your belongings."

Ms. Whitford sat down on the arm of the recliner and poured the tea. "Now that we understand each other, I need you to do exactly what I tell you. This applies to when you are here writing and when you are at home training Scrum and doing your assignments for me. What you do with your time between will be up to you. But I need you to promise me you will come here every day, write what I tell you to write, and train your dragon according to my rules. No excuses. No matter what happens in the rest of your young life, you must follow my instructions perfectly. And, Polly…"

"Yes, Ms. Whitford."

Ms. Whitford looked at Polly over her glasses. "No writing outside of your time with me, unless I tell you."

"What about essays and stuff at school?"

"Do your school work, but nothing on your own." She glanced at the back of Polly's hand. "No more scribbling on yourself either."

Polly opened her mouth to protest.

"Not a word."

Polly covered her hand.

Ms. Whitford sipped her tea. "Good. Then let's begin at the beginning."

Ms. Whitford went to a glass bookcase near the door, opened it, and took a book out. She handed Polly a first-edition, 1952 copy of *Charlotte's Web* by E.B. White. "I want you to understand the business of publishing is just that: a business. And, like any other business, a publishing company has to make and sell a product at a profit. I know it's hard to think of publishing like a pet supply business, for instance, but that's all it really is.

"Let's imagine I own a factory that makes toothpaste for dogs, and you are my sales person. If I send you to a clothing store to sell our dog toothpaste, do you think the owner of the clothing store will buy it from us?"

"No."

"What if I send you to a pet store? Do you think the owner would buy our toothpaste for dogs?"

"Sure."

"It's the same with poems, short stories, scripts, novels, and any kind of writing, fiction or non-fiction. The writer is the factory. The writer produces the product— widgets made of words called manuscripts—and tries to sell her widgets to the appropriate middle-man." Ms. Whitford pointed at the leather-bound manuscript on her desk.

"Now a manuscript like this one is not ready for sale to readers. It's just pages of text, unbound, with no book jacket. As a writer, I have to sell my manuscript to a book publisher. The book publisher spends a great deal of money editing, proofreading, formatting, designing, and printing multiple copies of my book. But the work does not end there. The publisher has to market and sell my book to booksellers, who then have to market and sell my book to readers."

Polly was getting lost. She had never thought of publishing as a business before. She was struck by the coldness of it. It seemed strange and unnatural somehow that writing was about making money and not about the work itself.

"Imagine this scenario, Polly. Let's say a man named Billy Bradley writes a young adult mystery novel, and he sends it to a publisher who specializes in selling children's picture books. If you were the person at the publishing company who reviewed at all the manuscripts coming in, would you recommend to your boss that he make a cash offer for Billy Bradley's mystery novel?"

"I don't think my boss would want to spend a bunch of money making a type of book we didn't sell. I'd probably get fired."

"Right. Each company, even the really big ones, has it's own type of work it knows it can sell. They rarely take chances on something new or on something that's outside the proven genres they know will turn a profit. It costs a lot of money to turn a manuscript into a book that can go on bookstore shelves. It costs even more money to market the book so it sells a few thousand copies. And publishing company executives need to answer to their shareholders. Like every other business, they favour sure things. That's why when an author is a hit, publishers want the author to keep churning out books similar to the original bestseller.

"This is why so many authors with solidly written manuscripts do not find success publishing. They don't do their market research. They try to sell their manuscript to the wrong type of publishing company. Like you tried to sell our dog toothpaste to a clothing store. It makes no sense from a business owner's point of view."

"Is that the only reason writers don't get published?"

"Sadly, no," Ms. Whitford chuckled. "Even though some writers are able to train their dragons enough to finish a piece of writing, they often do not train them well enough to keep editing a piece of writing until it is truly ready for sale. Think of a first draft as a lump of clay, nothing more, but also nothing less. It's an accomplishment, but it's just a lump. It needs to be sculpted, decorated, glazed, and fired before it can go on display for sale.

"Writers who have not trained their dragons are often too impatient. They think their lump of clay is a ready-to-sell manuscript. They want glory today for a low investment of time and energy. Glory does not work that way. The publishing world is brutally, harshly competitive. It has no time or patience for wannabes. Writers have to take this seriously and think like businesspeople. You have to run your manuscript factory at full-steam and in perfect condition. Your dragon must be trained and be part of the process. Long hours, strained eyes, bleeding fingers, carpel tunnel syndrome. Hard work is absolutely necessary."

"Is it talent or hard work that matters more?"

"They are both important, but hard work matters more, and your dragon is critical to your success. The good news is the more often you work through the writing process—getting an idea, researching the idea, focusing the idea, writing your lump of clay, editing your lump of clay, proofreading, and formatting—the better trained your dragon will be, and the more efficient you will become at producing publishable pieces of writing."

Ms. Whitford picked up the golden urn she had shown Polly the previous day. It had a lid with a raised design on it. It was a relief of a muscular, broad-chested dragon with outstretched wings and open jaws. Polly had not noticed the dragon before. She handed the urn to Polly.

Polly gingerly accepted the urn. She couldn't take her eyes of the dragon and was dying to know what was inside.

Ms. Whitford said, "The other day you told me this was once a lump of clay, right?"

"Right," said Polly.

Ms. Whitford paced around the room as she continued. "Let's imagine we have a factory that makes funerary urns like this one." She stopped and looked at Polly, expecting a response. Polly just blinked at her, waiting to hear what she would say next.

"Polly, what steps are involved in making a funerary urn? If you were the factory operations manager, how would you produce these in an efficient and cost-effective manner?"

Polly thought for a moment as she held the urn up for closer examination. "We would need clay. Once the clay was kneaded, we would use a potter's wheel to shape it. Then we would sculpt the lid. Then we would paint it with glaze and fire it."

"Exactly!" said Ms. Whitford, taking the urn back. She returned it to the shelf and went to her desk, where she opened the deep bottom drawer and pulled out a red plastic egg. She opened the egg and showed Polly the pink putty inside. "I will give you this when the first draft of your manuscript is complete. Not before." Then she put the pink putty back in the plastic egg and put the egg back in her desk drawer.

"What manuscript? I don't get it." Polly had been sidetracked, wondering whether or not there were dragon ashes inside the golden urn, and had missed the point of the pink putty and why she would want it.

"Much like the urn has steps in its creation, so does a manuscript, any kind of manuscript. With me, you will be writing a short story. This will be the key to training your dragon. It is the perfect type of writing for you. It requires a great deal of discipline, but it's relatively quick to produce and highly marketable."

Polly groaned. Short stories were easy to start but impossible to finish. She started off okay, but along the way always seemed to convince herself the idea was big enough for a novel. Then she would keep writing until she got bored or the story just got away from her, and she dropped it.

"Not to worry, Polly. I'll be here to support you." Ms. Whitford smiled. "Back to the writing process. What steps would a writer take to go from having nothing but an idea to having a publishable manuscript of a short story?"

Polly struggled to remember what she had been taught in English class. "You get an idea. You do a draft. You do a good copy. Then you proofread it and send it in."

"That's a good guess, but not quite right. First, you need an idea. That is correct. But what you do with it?" Ms. Whitford sat down in the easy chair across from Polly and poured more tea for both of them.

Polly watched the steaming amber liquid tumble into her cup. "You think about it and figure out if it's a good idea or not."

Ms. Whitford shook her head. "No more thinking about it. You sit down and you write whatever comes out of you about the idea. You explore. You have fun. You write a few pages. If, as you are writing, you begin to visualize a story with an interesting main character with a relatable problem, you know you have a good idea for a story. The free writing of the details of your idea will awaken your imagination and allow the story to flow out of you. Do you think it would be wise to let a dragon like Scrum interfere with your writing at this early stage of the process?"

"Maybe."

"Never," said Ms. Whitford, clapping her hands loudly for emphasis. "You never let your dragon put his two cents in at this early step. If you do, your idea will become nothing more than an idea. Remember, your dragon is a talented but impatient amplifier of your weaknesses as a writer. He will rip you and your work to shreds and tell you that you will never make it. His criticisms will undermine your confidence and choke the flow of words, when you use him at the wrong time. You must get him under your control. He has to learn when he is needed and when he is not."

"What do I do with Scrum if I'm just writing my idea down and exploring and having fun like you say?"

"How about you do some writing for me now, and then I'll give you an exercise to do with your dragon tonight. Would you prefer to write or type?"

"Type." Polly turned around in the desk chair.

Ms. Whitford came over and jiggled the mouse. She opened a blank document for Polly. "I can't let you go until you have two good story ideas, so I'm going to give you some quick and dirty brainstorming exercises. You are going to choose two, and then you are going to sit down with Scrum tonight and do some writing."

A sharp thud made Polly and Ms. Whitford look up at the window. Fat drops of water were blowing sideways into the panes.

"Here's your first exercise, Polly." Ms. Whitford pulled a picture out of a shoebox filled to the brim with miscellaneous photographs, some colour, some black and white. She handed it to Polly. It was a picture of a German castle on a hill surrounded by soft-looking pale green trees. "Look at this photo and start writing whatever comes to mind: setting, character, plot, theme, anything. You have three minutes. Go."

Ms. Whitford made Polly repeat the exercise with four other photographs. Some of them were easy to write about and Polly had wished for more time, while others were difficult and Polly found it hard to fill three minutes with words. But, in the end, she had five chunks of writing and was ready to go home.

"Not yet," said Ms. Whitford.

Polly massaged her neck and stretched her fingers. She was feeling tired and getting hungry. "Okay," she agreed.

"What if a spider could weave a magical web and then used her webs to save a runty pig? What if a noble-man became king of Scotland in a devious manner and then went mad with guilt? What if a downtrodden teen-ager met her fairy godmother and was able to transform her life? Do you recognize any of these stories, Polly?"

Polly smiled. It was too easy. "*Charlotte's Web. Macbeth. Cinderella.*"

"Excellent."

Ms. Whitford then asked Polly to come up with five of her own "What if?" story ideas. It took Polly a while to complete, but she was pleased with her ideas until Ms. Whitford ran through them and said only one of them was suitable for a short story. The rest, she said, were better suited for novels or full-length, feature film scripts.

At the end of their session, Polly had two ideas out of the ten she felt she could write about, and Ms. Whitford had approved. Her first idea was from the third photo she had written about in the first exercise: a picture of a little girl riding a merry-go-round. Polly liked that the photo had been taken while the merry-go-round was running, which blurred the horses and the lights slightly. She began the exercise by simply writing down words to describe the merry-go-round, but the words soon turned into sentences about a girl who ran away from home to join the circus. Three minutes had gone by too quickly.

Her second idea was from the "What if?" exercise. She had come up with this statement: *What if a girl discovered a dragon and then used the dragon to became a famous author?*

CHAPTER SIX

A Big Nuisance

Polly leaned against the remnants of her room, which were still heaped against the bedroom window. A dozen empty pencil packages were on the floor, strewn around her outstretched legs. Scrum lay across the room from her, his long back against the wall in pasty coils. He rested his hairy chin on the floor and seemed to be dozing. Polly was ready to give up.

The task had seemed simple. All she had to do was sit in her room with Scrum and write at least two pages for each of her story ideas. She was to write playfully, saying yes to everything her imagination threw at her, without any commentary or criticism from Scrum. But, it was nearing midnight, and she had not been able to write a word without Scrum peering over her shoulder, telling her what a lousy writer she was and how bad her ideas were. She had tried bribing him to be quiet with pencils, but it only kept him silent for the split second it took for him to swallow. Though, now, he looked like he was going to sleep for the rest of the night.

Polly sighed and looked down at her open notebook. She had been at it since after dinner, which had ended unusually early because her mom had wanted to hear the details of Polly's appointment with Dr. Mammozarack. Polly, not wanting to talk about it, had rushed silently through her lasagne and excused herself saying she had a lot of homework to do and would tell her mom about it in the morning.

"Ugh!" Polly threw her notebook and pencil at Scrum. They bounced off his white scales. "Why did you eat my computer? I can't write on paper!"

Scrum lifted an eyelid and looked at Polly. His one-eyed glare made Polly think about her appointment with Dr. Mammozarack. Letting it creep back into her thoughts made her shudder. It had been the longest fifty-five minutes of her life.

The doctor had seemed civil enough when Polly first arrived in the tidy office. There was a bookcase filled with thick dictionaries, an abstract metal sculpture in a corner, and a large framed print of pandas eating bamboo shoots on the wall behind her desk. It all seemed normal enough at the beginning. Dr. Mammozarack had asked Polly why she thought she was there. Polly had replied simply, "Because my dad just moved out and my parents think I'm really upset. But I'm fine."

Then, the tone of the session had changed. Dr. Mammozarack started asking Polly umpteen questions about pets. Did she have pets? Had she ever had a pet? Why not? Did she want a pet? What kind? If she had a pet what would she do with it? How would she train it? What would she feed it? How would she discipline it? Would she be cruel or kind? What would its name be? Polly began to get a sick feeling her mom had told the doctor about the "imaginary" dragon in her room.

Sensing something was amiss, Polly had shoved thoughts of Scrum out of her head and used a ferret in all her answers. It was the first animal that had popped into her head because Natasha had told her about a cute book she had been assigned to read in Life Skills class. It was a novel about a ferret who has to make a lot of money to save his family from being sold to a taxidermist.

Even worse, when the interrogation was over, Polly was almost stabbed as she hurried out through the waiting room. The doctor's next patient—a distracted, lanky boy about the same age as Polly—walked into to her while he was carving a small piece of pale wood with a pocket knife. His eyes were fixed on his work, and he barely looked up when he bumped into her. By the time he mumbled, "I'm sorry," Polly was already out the door and out of earshot. Fortunately, the knife had only nicked her school bag, but the whole experience had been awful. Polly did not want to ever see Dr. Mammozarack or the boy again.

"What are you staring at?" Polly asked Scrum.

Scrum lifted his hairy chin and sniffed at the pencil Polly had tossed at him. He snorted, "Give me something good to eat. No more pencils!"

"Give me back my laptop, and I'll give you something good to eat."

Scrum unfolded his wings sharply, making Polly's hair blow off her face.

Polly got up and rummaged around in the wreckage of her personal possessions.

"There's nothing yummy left in this entire room," said Scrum, "not a chip, not a wire. You'll have to go out and buy me some laptops. Wake me up when you get back." He yawned, folded his wings, and closed his eyes. Soon, he was snoring.

Polly dug through the remnants until she found what she was looking for, a gift box from her twelfth birthday. It had been crushed during one of Scrum's rages, but the contents were still inside. It held some of her first attempts at writing, all on scraps of candy wrappers and crumpled pieces of lined paper from school. It also contained a few additional treasures like her eraser collection from elementary school and her first computer mouse. The mouse was pink and had a princess on it. It was all that remained of the princess computer her dad had given her when she started kindergarten. She had never used it to write, but she had, for a while, called the pink mouse "Charlotte" and made a nest for it on the floor beside her bed.

Laura Michelle Thomas

Polly went over to the snoring dragon and hit him on the snout. "I want my laptop back." She dangled Charlotte, the pink computer mouse, in front of his nose.

Scrum snorted and puffed and shook his big head. He was dazed and angry. "I was dreaming. How dare you awaken a sleeping dragon!" Scrum caught the scent of the mouse and inhaled loudly. "Yum. Better than pencils." He licked his lips eagerly.

Polly quickly put the mouse behind her back. "Not until you give me back my laptop."

"Give me the yummy thing, and I will give it back to you." He opened his jaws wide.

Polly could see down the black pipe of his throat. The smell curled her eyebrow hairs. She plugged her nose. "Give me my laptop first."

Scrum started to laugh. "It's gone for good, and the world can thank me later. Your story ideas are dreadful, so cliché. A girl runs away to join the circus, and a girl trains a dragon. Those have to be two of the worst story ideas I have ever heard. If you can be a writer, I can be a hummingbird." Scrum hummed and flapped his wings as he pranced around the room.

When Polly flushed red, Scrum laughed so hard he couldn't hum anymore. He was truly enjoying himself.

Polly picked up her notebook and left the room, closing the door quietly behind her so she wouldn't wake her mom. As she stood in the hallway, her back against the door, she listened to the dragon roar with laughter.

When he stopped and noticed Polly was gone, she heard him call out, his voice rising with panic. "Where did she go? I'm hungry. I need her to come back. I need that mouse. I didn't mean it. Please come back."

Polly could hear him snuffling and snorting on the other side of the door.

"Come back in, please. Your story ideas are...please... come back. I'm sorry I ate your laptop. I won't do it again."

Polly opened the door slightly and took a step inside.

Scrum made his move. He pushed the door all the way open and knocked Polly to the floor, sending Charlotte flying through the air. It landed on Scrum's pale pink tongue, and he swallowed it with a single satisfied gulp. Belching, he strode over to his nest, wormed his way inside, and disappeared.

Polly sat down where her bed used to be and found a black ballpoint pen. She really wanted to write something but was too discouraged to work on her story ideas. Scrum was right; they were dumb ideas. She moved the pen just above her left hand imagining how good it would feel to let the ink roll across her skin, but she resisted the urge. She had made a promise to Ms. Whitford, and she intended to keep it.

*

Polly sat in the cafeteria at school with Natasha. There was a new boy in their grade who turned out to be the lanky boy from the doctor's office. Polly could not believe her bad luck and that she had not recognized him in the first place. She wanted to go over and kick him in the shins once for making a hole in her school bag and twice for not looking like his picture on the inside cover of all his books.

The boy's name was Yulleg Snoblivski, and his family had just moved into the biggest mansion in the richest part of town. All the kids at Polly's school knew who Yulleg Snoblivski was, even the jocks and the boys in shop class. By age five, Yulleg had already written his first novel. By age ten, he had written six screen plays, seventeen more novels, and two works of poetry that literary critics said rivaled Shakespeare's sonnets. With his latest book, *Dragon by a Tale*, which was due to be released worldwide in time for summer vacation, Yulleg was on track to be the the only author to simultaneously win every international book prize awarded in a single year, including the Nobel Prize for Literature. Some of

　　　　　　　Laura Michelle Thomas

the kids said the Snoblivski family was now one of the wealthiest families in the world.

"He's cute," whispered Natasha, as Yulleg maneuvered his tray of food around a gaggle of girls from the school book club. The girls held out their hands and begged him for an autograph, promising never to wash again.

Polly's cheeks flushed with embarrassment. She had asked for the complete Yulleg Snoblivski collection for Christmas and had not received it. Her mom said it was sold out by the time she had gone to the store to buy it. Now here he was at her school.

"He's...he's a...he's a rogue whittler!" she said.

Natasha looked at Polly. "What are you babbling about?"

"He likes to whittle—you know, use a knife to make art out of wood. He made a hole in my bag and just about stabbed me yesterday at..." Polly hesitated.

"Where?" asked Natasha.

"Nowhere. Maybe it wasn't him. I bumped into a guy who was carving a piece of wood while he was walking. So rude and dangerous. I thought it was him. Yuck! He's not cute." The steep angle of the boy's profile reminded her of Dr. Mammozarack.

"No way! He's totally cute."

"You already said that." Polly was highly irritated by Yulleg and his fawning fans, including Natasha.

"Yeah..." said Natasha. She was outright staring at the boy.

The bell rang.

"Too bad. No lunch for poor Yulleg." Polly smirked at the full tray of food that had been parked on a table while Yulleg signed autographs.

Natasha stood up, beaming. "I know! I'll give him my granola bar before English. He's in our class."

"Great." Polly picked up her open notebook. She had written a thin paragraph for each story idea that morning while sitting on the toilet in the girl's washroom. It was far less than the two pages than Ms. Whitford had asked her to write, but at least it was something.

"What are you writing, a sonnet for Yulleg so he'll give you a signed copy of *Dragon by a Tale* when it comes out?"

Polly glared at her friend.

"I was just kidding. What's gotten into you? You're so touchy."

"Dragons! I'm just sick and tired of everybody talking about stupid, ugly dragons."

Natasha shrugged and placed a hand on Polly's shoulder. "I'm really sorry about your parents."

"Oh, whatever!" said Polly, shrugging away Natasha's hand. "Let's go to English and see what this guy has that we don't."

Laura Michelle Thomas

CHAPTER SEVEN

Literary Dragons

Ms. Whitford was dressed all in black, and, from what Polly could tell, her mood suited it. "You say your mother is sending you to see Dr. Miriam Mammozarack for counselling about some kind of a mental breakdown because of your your father leaving and your parents' separation."

"Yes." Polly wondered where the friendly teapot was.

Ms. Whitford exhaled a low whistle. "That is a name I haven't heard since about the time you were born." She paused. "And you saw the writing prodigy, Yulleg Snoblivski, author of the soon-to-be-released *Dragon by a Tale*, at her office as you left, and you think he was her next patient."

"Yes. He almost stabbed me because he was whittling a piece of wood while he walked."

"Whittling? How bizarre." Ms. Whitford stopped pacing and sat down heavily in her office chair. "Do you see the urn we talked about last time?"

Polly looked over at the bookshelf. It was the golden one with the raised dragon image on the lid, the one that had once been a lump of clay. She nodded.

"Yulleg's father was a writer named Johan."

"Yulleg's dad is a writer too?"

"Was a writer. He's dead."

"But I heard at school that Yulleg lives with his mom and dad."

"His mother gave Yulleg up for adoption when he was an infant, just days after he was born."

"Really?"

Ms. Whitford nodded. "Johan, Yulleg's biological father, did his training at the same time I did. He died unexpectedly when we were young adults, and Johan's dragon didn't die like he was supposed to. The dragon's name is Felix, and Felix's ashes should be in that golden urn, but they are not. Felix is now Yulleg's dragon."

Polly thought for a moment. "Yulleg Snoblivski has a dragon?"

"Of course! Every writer has one."

"Good for Yulleg, then! He's got his father's dragon." Polly was enraged with jealousy because Yulleg had a dragon more mature and, evidently, more powerful than hers. "You should see the girls falling over him at school. It's painful to watch."

Ms. Whitford closed her eyes and sighed. "I'm sorry. I forgot to make tea. How impolite of me." She opened her eyes again and studied Polly closely. "I'm going to have to tell you some things that might be hard for you to understand so early in your training."

Polly bit her lower lip. "Okay."

Ms. Whitford went over to the bookcase and picked up Felix's urn. She opened it and showed Polly it was empty. "For millennia, storytellers and writers have been born with inner dragons locked deep inside them. The dragons always—how shall I say it?—pop out of their writers during the teen years or even into adulthood. But never before puberty, at least, not under normal circumstances. Literary dragons, as they are officially called, are dangerous until their writers have learned how and when to use them. This is why I am training you to handle Scrum. If I don't, the consequences could be disastrous."

Polly wished the tea things were already out. "I don't understand."

"In the early days, back before anyone really understood the relationship between literary dragons and their writers, we lost many talented individuals. Many writers lost their minds and were locked up in asylums or exiled from their villages because they couldn't figure out how to live with their dragons. Some even took their own lives. It is tragic that so many writers and so many stories have been lost forever.

"For a long time the world's stories were told only by a few powerful storytellers; these were powerful men and women who figured out how to control their dragons, how to work with them, how to use them to serve their literary careers. This is not how it should be. The world needs many stories told by many writers, from a multitude of perspectives. I truly believe every aspiring writer with a literary dragon inside needs to have the opportunity to let his or her words enter deeply into the world. Monolithic master-narratives are the enemy of freedom. History has shown us what can happen when book burning and author arrests become part of a society's theme."

Polly licked her lips and wondered if her stories were truly as important as Ms. Whitford seemed to think.

Ms. Whitford ran a hand across her brow to sweep away a few loose tendrils of hair. "I'll get the tea things shortly. I am getting thirsty too." She pushed her glasses farther up the bridge of her nose. "Fortunately, the writers who were able to train their dragons in those early days formed a guild, one in which the members pledged to help new writers train their dragons. I am part of that guild. So was Yulleg's father." Ms. Whitford put Felix's urn back on the bookshelf.

Polly was confused. "But dragons cannot live without their writers. How can Felix be Yulleg's dragon, and what really happened to Yulleg's father? Maybe he is still alive, and that's why Felix is alive."

Ms. Whitford shook her head slowly. "No. Johan is dead. The Guild knows that for certain. What we don't know is how Felix was able to escape death when his writer died, or how he was able to bond with Yulleg. This has never happened before. The story in writing circles is that Felix popped out of Yulleg when the boy was just three years old, which of course explains how he was able to write his first novel by age five. But nothing about it is natural. We don't know if Yulleg even had his own dragon to begin with."

Polly leaned back in the recliner and looked up at the coffered ceiling. "But who is the writer? Is it Felix or Yulleg?"

"Whether the stories are Felix's or Yulleg's or a combination, I don't know. The Guild does not know. Yulleg is a rogue. He is not a member of the Guild so we have kept our distance, perhaps for too long." Ms. Whitford paused. "To answer your question about where the stories come from, usually it's the writer who comes up with ideas. The writer writes a first draft of a manuscript—a lump of clay—and then uses his or her literary dragon to turn those ideas into a publishable piece of writing. However, there is nothing usual or natural about the bond between Yulleg and Felix, so I cannot say where the lines are drawn or who is in control. I do believe it's high time the Guild brought them both in for questioning."

Polly looked at Ms. Whitford. "What is Yulleg's new book about?"

"We don't know. Mightright, the publishing company that handles Yulleg's books, has not done its usual preproduction marketing campaign. All they have released is the title, *Dragon by a Tale*. They could be growing complacent about Yulleg's success, or they are trying to capitalize on it and build up the suspense. There is something suspicious about the secrecy, and now that I know Miriam Mammozarack is somehow involved with Yulleg..." Ms. Whitford drummed her fingers on her thighs.

"Does Yulleg know what's happening? I mean he can see his dragon, Felix, right? Like I can see Scrum."

"Yes."

Laura Michelle Thomas

"And what about Dr. Mammozarack?"

"She and I were colleagues, once upon a time. I was never friends with her. Johan was the only Guild member who got along with her. After he died, she quit her training as a writer, left the Guild, and did a doctorate in some kind of engineering."

Polly blurted out, "I didn't do my homework the way you wanted me to."

"I know. You suffer from a bad case of writer's block just like I did when I was your age. My mother used to call it two things: procrastinationitis and wordophobia. But, really, writer's block is just a symptom of not knowing when and how to use your literary dragon." Ms. Whitford stood up.

"I'll go make tea. It will give you ten minutes to write. Spend five minutes on each story. There is a timer on my desk. That will be your warm up today." Ms. Whitford paused in the doorway as she watched Polly set up at the desk and flip over the timer.

Polly didn't need to be told twice. She put her brain in full-gear and let her imagination light up like a movie screen. By the time Ms. Whitford was back with the tea, Polly had typed up a full page on each story idea, single spaced. The printer hummed and spat out her work.

Ms. Whitford's face brightened. "Terrific! Now, which one of these ideas do you think is better suited to the short story genre and why?"

Polly really couldn't tell. They both seemed pretty good to her. "Either one."

Ms. Whitford took both sheets and gave them a quick read. "Let's talk about what a short story is and what it isn't." Ms. Whitford took a collection of short stories off one of the bookshelves and handed it to Polly. "What is a short story?"

Polly thought for a moment. "It's a short piece of writing, like an article or essay. Maybe anything shorter than a novel?"

"How long do you think a story can be before it's no longer a short story but a novella or novel?"

"Five thousand words?" Polly guessed, thumbing through the book.

"Possibly, if you want to get published in a literary journal or trade magazine. But much longer stories were once highly marketable as short stories—back in the old days, before TVs and computers. Technically, a story can be up to 25,000 words long and still be considered a short story. If you are writing 250 words per manuscript page, that's one hundred pages. Anything over 25,000 words and under about 45,000 words can be considered a novella. Anything over 45,000 gets you into novel territory. What else do you think makes a short story a short story and not some other genre of writing?"

Polly shrugged. She hadn't really thought about it before.

"A short story is fictional. It is written in prose, not poetry. And, it has a narrative structure with a beginning, middle, and end." Ms. Whitford took the collection of short stories back from Polly and continued. "What do you think makes a great short story?"

"A great title?"

"All the short stories in this book have something in common."

"Are they all about the same topic?"

"Not even close. They tackle a whole range of subjects." Ms. Whitford opened the book and showed Polly the table of contents. "Each short story in this collection has depth and unity. That is the difference between a short story that is publishable and one that is not—depth and unity."

"What's unity?"

"It's when everything works together around a single theme and title..." Ms. Whitford's voice trailed off.

Polly nodded and glanced at her story ideas. She had titles in mind for both of them and was about to tell Ms. Whitford what they were, but Ms. Whitford surfaced from her thoughts and said, "I haven't given you your training exercises for today...and time is...with Yulleg

Laura Michelle Thomas

and Miriam working together—I have people I need to contact."

"Should I just leave?" Polly wished at that moment she could just walk out the door and get her old life back. What did she know about guilds and dragons and urns without ashes?

Ms. Whitford looked at Polly, her brown furrowed. "No, Polly. You are too important to the story now."

"Me? What? How?"

"I don't know yet," sighed Ms. Whitford. "I wish I did." The writer shook her head as if to shake herself back into the present moment. "Here is your homework. Write this down on the back of one of your stories."

Polly flipped over the paper that had her dragon story idea on it and prepared to take notes.

"You are going to read each of your story ideas out loud to Scrum. He will, by nature, interrupt you constantly and tell you your idea is bad. Only he will not be so polite. But I would like you to persist. Talk over him. Do not stop reading until you have finished both stories. Then you are to take this muzzle and put it over his snout." Ms. Whitford handed Polly a large leather muzzle.

Polly waved it away. "I can't put that on him."

"You can and you will."

Polly accepted the muzzle. Though it was bulky, it was amazingly light in her hands. It also had a layer of fabric on the inside, which was extremely soft. She rubbed it with her thumb. "Is this velvet?"

"The lining was made from the fleece of a wooly mammoth. It won't hurt Scrum, but he will fight you when you try to put it on. But you must get it on before doing the next part of your exercise. Now write this down, please."

Polly put the muzzle on the desk beside her two sheets of paper.

"Once you have the muzzle on him," Ms. Whitford continued, "you will review each story quietly to yourself and determine which is better suited to the short story genre. Once you decide which story is the one you are going to write, you will look at Scrum straight in the eyes—don't be afraid to get right up nose-to-nose with him—and tell him why the idea is perfectly suited for a two-thousand word short story. Then, and only then, you will take the muzzle off, give him a treat, and do some writing. Scrum should remain silent so you can write in peace."

"Do I write my whole story?" Polly twisted the leather in her hands.

"No. Write three paragraphs for me. Write one describing your main character, one describing your plot from beginning to end, and one describing your main setting. This is the second step in the writing process—research."

"You mean like going to the library?"

"Yes, and to the Internet. You can also do interviews or look at photos. There are many sources outside of a writer's imagination that can be used to develop a story world and make it believable. I know we are writing fiction when we write a short story, but it has to be believable. Where else can you go for research?"

"Memories?"

"Exactly right. Remember it will always be easier to describe settings, characters, and situations you are familiar with. That is why so many of the great writers travelled and then were able to write exotic settings and situations that were fictional but seemed so real. They looked out their windows on the Mediterranean or on the African savannah and described what they actually saw and experienced. Where have you been?"

"Actually, I've never been anywhere," Polly shrugged. "My dad is the one who travels. He's been to every continent now, or at least every continent with big farms. He's a tractor salesman."

Ms. Whitford looked away from Polly with a pained expression on her face.

Polly was about to ask Ms. Whitford what was wrong, when the writer cleared her throat and continued. "So...

Laura Michelle Thomas

step two of the writing process is doing research, which can mean anything from an Internet search to diving into your personal experiences to create believable characters who have believable problems in believable settings. They don't have to be real, but they have to be believable. Nothing can break the spell—but I'm getting ahead of myself. Do you think we do any writing in step two?"

"Maybe just some notes?"

"Yes. That is a good place to start, but actually you should continue writing. You have to get your story out of your head and onto paper. Trust me, your dragon is not going to type it up and email it to you in perfectly formatted, double-spaced pages of Times New Roman 12-point font with one-inch margins. Do you think Scrum is going to do that for you? Hand you a polished, perfectly formatted manuscript?"

"Well...ah..."

"Never! That's not his job; it's yours!"

Polly just looked at Ms. Whitford, who was getting so animated that tendrils of hair were coming loose and waving across her round face.

"As I was saying, Polly. You need to write at the research step of the process. Maybe you write a scene with a focus on describing the setting. Or, you write a character sketch, or you just keep going with your manuscript. You need to write, freely, just like in step one. And you help Scrum learn when to keep his comments to himself with that." She pointed to the muzzle in Polly's hands.

Someone knocked at the front door several times in short, sharp succession. "And so it begins." Ms. Whitford frowned. "Take the muzzle and your homework and go out through the back garden."

"What about my bike? It's by the front door."

Ms. Whitford thought for a moment. "You'll have to leave it."

The knocking grew to banging.

Polly followed Ms. Whitford to the back door.

"One last thing." Ms. Whitford turned to face Polly. "Stay away from Yulleg and Dr. Mammozarack.

"But Yulleg is in my English class, and my mom is going to make me see her again. I know it."

"Do you best, then. Just keep your head down, do your writing exercises, and come back tomorrow. Now, go!"

Polly ran through the adjoining yards all the way to the street where the townhouse complex ended. She took one last look back to see if she could see Ms. Whitford's visitors. She couldn't, so she stuffed the muzzle in her school bag and started the long walk home. If she was lucky, she would never see Yulleg or the sharp-faced doctor again.

Laura Michelle Thomas

CHAPTER EIGHT

The Clinic

Polly sat in the waiting room of Dr. Mammozarack's office with her mom.

"I don't want to see this lady again. Seriously, Mom. She wasn't nice, and I don't feel any better after talking to her. She's—"

Polly's mom sighed sharply. "I don't know if it's drugs, or if you're falling into a depression brought on by the separation, but we have to take dragon hallucinations seriously. I think it's a good idea for you to spend the next few days getting some intensive therapy, as Dr. Mammozarack is suggesting."

Polly didn't answer. How could she tell her mom about the Guild, literary dragons, and Yulleg's mysterious book? How could she explain that the doctor was somehow involved?

"What are you thinking about now, more dragons?"

Polly shrugged. "I was just thinking about the night Dr. Mammozarack came to the apartment."

Her mom's face grew serious, and she took Polly's hands in her own. "The night you told me you had a dragon in your room, what about it?"

"Polly!" said the receptionist. "Dr. Mammozarack will see you and your mom now."

Dr. Mammozarack came out of her office smiling. "Welcome back, Polly. Follow me please."

Polly obediently followed the former Guild member and colleague of Ms. Whitford to her office. She wondered what the doctor was doing with Yulleg Snoblivski and how she was involved in *Dragon by a Tale*.

While Polly was wondering, Dr. Mammozarack handed a glossy brochure to her mom and began discussing the logistics of checking Polly into Dr. Mammozarack's depression clinic for teen girls that evening.

Polly's knees went weak. It felt as if the floor was falling out from beneath her feet as she watched her mom nod, smile, and agree with everything the doctor was saying.

Polly backed toward the open door. "Mom, no. I'm okay, really."

"Sit down, please," said Dr. Mammozarack. She ushered Polly to a chair and closed the door. Polly thought she heard the the sound of a lock clicking into place.

Polly looked at her mom. She could tell her mind was made up. "Can we at least go home so I can pack?" she pleaded.

Polly's mom said firmly, "Your suitcase is already in the car."

"You went in my room? How did you find my things? It's such a mess."

Dr. Mammozarack chuckled. "All the girls say that. I bet your room is neat as a pin. Isn't that right?" She glanced at Polly's mom.

She replied, "Not one thing out of place and no albino dragons, either."

The women laughed together, their voices bouncing around Polly as she sat in a black vinyl chair in the far corner of the office. She stared blankly at the print of the bamboo-eating pandas hanging on the wall behind Dr. Mammozarack's desk. She felt like the pandas—trapped

Laura Michelle Thomas

in the painting, mute, frozen, and powerless to stop what was going to happen next.

Less than an hour later on the outskirts of the city, in the stark lobby of Dr. Mammozarack's depression clinic for teen girls, Polly hugged her mom goodbye and watched her walk out through the clinic's tinted glass doors.

"Are you Polly?" asked a no-nonsense nurse in a crisp, pale pink uniform.

Polly nodded.

"Bring your suitcase and come with me."

Polly followed silently as the nurse talked non-stop. She ran through the clinic's many rules and regulations as they wove their way through a blurry series of long white hallways. Polly was so disheartened by the severe emptiness of the clinic and her separation from Scrum, she barely listened.

The nurse stopped in front of a white door barely perceptible in the wall and swung it open. "Here we are. I hope you understand everything I've explained to you. This is going to be your home for the next week, Polly. It's extremely important you do as you are told."

Polly nodded. Her arms were tired from carrying her suitcase. Her mom must have packed a clean outfit and a different pair of shoes for each day.

Though sparsely furnished with just a single bed, a dresser, and a small television, the room was clean and tidy. On the far side of the bed there was a large window. Polly went over to it and looked for a way to get it open. There was no latch. Worse, Polly was alarmed to see they were several stories up. "I don't remember coming up any stairs. I'm sure we went down some. Didn't we?"

The nurse crossed the room and looked over Polly's shoulder. "All the girls say that when they arrive. It's the shock of realizing your family has left and you are on your own. You girls never notice your surroundings because you live inside your heads. We're going to help you break that nasty little habit during your stay with us.

You'll see. We will make you happy again. Now, let me explain the schedule."

"Can I go down there?" Polly pointed to the court-yard below. In the centre was a rectangular pool about the length and width of a school bus. The greying bricks that edged the pool were rough, worn, and uneven. The water did not come all the way up to the top of the bricks, leaving a thick lip between the surface and the courtyard floor. The water was dark and reflected the side of the building on its indigo surface. Polly could not tell how deep it was.

"No, you may not. I told you that on the way here. The courtyard and reflecting pool are for staff only. The area is strictly off-limits to patients. Now, about the schedule..."

As the nurse carried on, Polly only half-listened. She missed her bedroom at home, destroyed though it was, and she definitely missed Scrum. She worried he would starve to death without her there to feed him. This made her think about the muzzle in her school bag. There had been no time to try it when she got home. Her mom had whisked her into the car as soon as she had walked through the door.

The nurse finished her speech. "Dinner—and your first therapy session—will be in the dining hall at sunset sharp."

"How will I know when it's sunset?" Polly craned her neck to look up. "I can barely see the sky from here."

"Rain or shine, a bell will chime five minutes before the sun goes down. When it does, please make your way down to the dining hall. I will not be there, but the others will."

"Others?" Polly turned away from the window to speak to the nurse, but she was already gone. "Great," she said aloud.

Polly tipped over her suitcase and sat down on it.
"Get off!"
Polly jumped up.
"Let me out!"

Polly whirled around. It was Scrum's voice, but the room was empty. "Where are you?" she asked.

"In here."

Polly put her suitcase flat on the floor and unzipped it. "Scrum?"

"I think I'm under your underwear."

Polly pulled out the clothes her mom had packed for her and piled them in a heap on the polished floor beside the suitcase. Underneath her underwear, she found her grandmother's antique mirror. She put it down on the floor, knelt down, and looked into it. "Are you in there?"

"Move! Look out!"

Polly rolled away from the mirror just as Scrum flew through the mirror and into the room. He looked as pale and bony as ever but was grinning from ear to ear. "That was fun. It was the first time I used my wings like that."

"Like what?"

"To fly. There was a tunnel with a light that led me here. Did you see how fast I flew? I can't wait to go outside. I've never been out there. Imagine flying out there!" Scrum looked past Polly to the window. "I'm starving. There was nothing to eat in there, but it smelled delicious."

"Where was there?"

"It wasn't my cave or the bedroom. It was all blackness and emptiness, with a lovely smell," he said, "but nothing to eat."

Polly looked at the small television on top of the dresser. "That might make a good snack."

Scrum sniffed the television, then inhaled it with a gulp. Polly cringed as she watch it slide under the blanched scales of his long neck. "Don't you chew?"

"That's better." Scrum belched as he looked around. "Where am I, and when do I get to go outside? I can't wait to feel the wind on my wings."

"We're at a clinic, and we need to get out of here."

Scrum looked at Polly and blinked, then he started sniffing around the room. "Something smells delicious. Better than TV."

"I didn't bring you any pencils..." Polly paused as a thought came to her. "Scrum, who packed my bag?"

"Your mother."

"Why did she pack the mirror?"

"She didn't."

"Who did?"

"I don't know. One minute I was in my cozy nest, and the next I was in a black place filled with nothing, and then when I saw the light I flew—it was wonderful. Then I was here with you."

Polly went to her suitcase and dumped all the contents on the bed. It was all clothes, nightgowns, shoes, and toiletries. Polly sifted through the contents until something caught her eye: strange, square lumps were showing through the lining at the bottom of the suitcase. She made a hole with her nail clippers and tore open the fabric. She found dozens of packages of pencils and six new computer mice, which someone had already taken out of their packages, along with the fleece muzzle and her notebook. Polly smiled. "I've got work to do Scrum, and I'm going to need you to cooperate."

She turned around slowly and presented the muzzle. "It's nice and soft, and you only have to wear it for a few minutes."

Scrum backed away from Polly. "You're not putting that torture device on me. I have a right to speak my mind. I will not be silenced."

"It's just for a few minutes. I already know what story I am going to write for Ms. Whitford. I just need you to be quiet for a few seconds. Let's try it." She held the clasp open and took a step toward him.

"Never!" Scrum extended his neck to its full length, which put his head near the ceiling. Polly had no way of reaching his face and knew there was no point trying to wrestle him into submission.

Laura Michelle Thomas

Polly tucked the muzzle under her arm and broke open a package of pencils. "How about a snack?"

Scrum shook his head and rolled his eyes. "I don't know why you think you can write. You have to be really smart to do that, and you are a dumb as glue. What's this story you want to write for Ms. Whitford anyway? Is it the one about the sad circus girl?"

"I'll tell you once you let me put this on."

Scrum approached Polly. "Sure."

She relaxed and held the muzzle open. This was going to be easier than she thought.

Scrum came right up to Polly with his eyes blinking meekly and his head bowed. But then things went terribly wrong.

Just as his head was close enough for Polly to slip the muzzle over his snout, he began to curl his long, white body loosely around her. "What if I promise not to talk while you tell me about your story?" he hissed as he tightened the coils. "Will you throw that evil thing out the window?"

Polly pushed at Scrum's scale-covered flesh, but she wasn't strong enough to stop the increasing pressure. The pencils she held snapped in half, and the muzzle was crushed between her body and the dragon's.

Scrum glared at Polly with his pink eyes and began to squeeze so hard Polly struggled to draw air into her chest.

"You can't kill me," she squeaked. "Literary dragons can't live without their writers. Didn't they teach you anything in your cave?"

Scrum's pink eyes narrowed. "I might not be able to kill you, but I can take you so close to death you will never try to use that torture device on me again."

"I...I..." Polly opened her mouth wide and gasped for air, but she couldn't expand her chest wide enough to draw another breath. She started to panic and began to struggle against Scrum with all the strength she had left in her.

The dragon held tight.

Just when she thought she was going to lose consciousness, Scrum relaxed. Polly dropped to the floor gasping for air and stayed there, panting on all fours like a dog until she could draw enough breath to form words.

"Here's my idea for the story." Polly sat up and propped her back against the bed. She breathed heavily and rubbed her ribs, which felt bruised.

"You may continue," said Scrum, laying like a sultan against the far wall, "now that we have reached an understanding."

Polly spoke, her lungs heaving out the words, "It's about a girl who wants to be a writer, and she finds a literary dragon and—"

"Wrong. Next idea."

Polly was too weak to put up a fight. At that moment, she understood why so many writers were driven insane by their dragons. She also understood why Ms. Whitford and the Guild were so important. She shuddered at the thought of a world where literary dragons were in control. Writers would be lost, and their stories lost with them.

Polly looked away from Scrum. "My story is about a girl who runs away from home to join the circus after her parents separate."

"Go on."

"I'm going to call it 'The Circus Girl.' The main character is a girl a bit younger than me, Pearl, who goes to the circus and meets a boy. He looks after the fun house—you know the attraction with all those mirrors that make you look funny. Pearl decides to go with him when the circus leaves town because things are bad at home. She's an only child. She and the boy travel around the world together and get married."

"Boring. Wake me up when you come up with something better." Scrum rolled his eyes before he closed them and started snoring.

Polly frowned.

A bell chimed.

Scrum raised his head and looked around the room.

Polly couldn't remember what the sound was for. She got up and looked down at the courtyard and reflecting pool. Dr. Mammozarack was there, her long arms jutting angrily away from her body as she spoke to a group of nurses. She kept pointing at the reflecting pool, and the nurses kept looking from the doctor to the pool. It was getting dark, but the water in the pool reflected sunset's orange glow.

"I think it's time for dinner," said Polly.

"What?" asked Scrum, who was partly rolled over on his back. His mid-section blocked the door.

"I need to go down to the dining hall for dinner."

Scrum got up and walked over to the window. He looked over Polly's head. "What's so interesting down there?"

"Nothing." Polly turned away from the window to leave, but she didn't sense Scrum's closeness and banged into him nose-first. "Ouch! Move, Scrum."

Without saying a word, but with a grin spread wide across his colourless face, Scrum stepped aside and let Polly pass. She held her sore nose and didn't look at him. He watched with interest as she left the room.

As soon as the door clicked shut, Scrum tore into the pencils and computer mice. He ate everything, belched loudly, then tried to decide which corner of the room would be the best place to take a nap.

Just as he was about to settle into the corner farthest away from the door, there was a polite knock. Scrum's tail twitched nervously. He did not know what to do. He had never answered a knock at the door before, so he froze, hoping whoever was there would either come in or go away.

The door opened gently. Scrum stiffened and prepared to attack, just in case it was Polly returning to put the muzzle back on him.

"Hello, dragon. I have a treat for you," said Dr. Mammozarack. She walked slowly into the room, carrying a brand new laptop under one arm.

Scrum inhaled deeply and licked his lips. The doctor placed the laptop on the floor and told Scrum to sit. He did.

She stood quietly. Scrum sat quietly, drooling.

Then the doctor snapped her fingers. "Eat!" she said.

Scrum licked up the laptop and swallowed it whole.

Dr. Mammozarack walked over to the bed and picked up two things—the mirror and the muzzle. "How quaint," she said in a honeyed voice. "Don't you worry, my lovely dragon. I have an easier way to train you."

Scrum smiled and licked his lips.

"Felix!" called Dr. Mammozarack, the honey gone from her voice.

A disfigured, ruddy creature the size of a chicken limped into the room. His head was almost as large as his body, and his scales were blotchy. Fleshy, red scars pockmarked his joints. Though he was a dragon, he had no beard and only one horn on the right side of his head. Where there should have been a second horn, on the left side, there was only a fleshy, waxen bump. You could tell the dragon once had wings, but they had been reduced to ragged flaps of burnt skin that hung from thick knobs on his back. His tail was a fleshy, dark-pink nub that twitched awkwardly when it moved.

"Give this young dragon a snack before his procedure. And see if you can figure out the source of that putrid smell. Maybe he needs a bath." The doctor turned sharply and walked out of the room.

Felix looked up at Scrum and scowled. "Don't stand there looking like a dummy, you noxious thing. You'll eat us out of this place, I'm sure. But the doctor wants me to give you a decent dragon meal and a bath, so follow me. And keep up! I don't have time to be mucking about with ignorant whelps like you. My writer is a superstar, you know. Yulleg Snoblivski. I'm sure you've heard of him!"

Scrum was too afraid to answer, so he just looked at the scabby little dragon and blinked.

　　　　　Laura Michelle Thomas

Felix snapped, "Just keep your snout shut and follow me."

Scrum followed Felix down a long hallway. Felix walked slowly and didn't say anything. Scrum followed, quietly dreaming about having a real dragon meal. Though he was anxious for Felix to pick up the pace, he didn't dare break the silence.

CHAPTER NINE

Therapy

The dining hall was vibrant white with black marble floors that reminded Polly of a freshly polished bowling ball. In the middle of the room, beneath a web-like metal and glass chandelier, sat an imposing glass table where nine girls sat typing on black and silver laptops. She did not recognize any of them, and they did not speak or look up as Polly was escorted to an empty chair on the far side of the table. Even when she sat down, Polly was too far away from the others to see what was on their screens. But, from the urgency of their typing and the earnestness of their expressions, she could tell they were writing something important. The pattering sound of nine girls typing resonated in the spacious hall as the nurse, who had met Polly at the entrance, left the room.

The table in front of Polly was empty. There was no computer, just the transparent surface of the glass table. She looked around to find a nurse or anyone who could tell her what she was supposed to be doing and when dinner would be served.

When a different nurse came into the hall, Polly put her hand up. The nurse opened a panel in the white wall, pressed a button, and exited without even glancing at Polly.

Polly heard a pop, followed by a clicking sound. She looked up. A black cylinder, the width of a hula hoop, was descending from the ceiling. It touched the glass, whirred for a minute, and began to retract, leaving behind a black and silver laptop like the others.

Polly glanced around the table. The delivery of Polly's laptop had not broken anyone's concentration. Not sure what else to do, she opened the laptop and pressed the power button.

A message flashed on the screen:

Hello, Polly. We know why your family sent you to us. You have a problem. You are depressed. You are depressed because you want to be a writer, when the truth is you do not have enough talent. Don't panic. During the next seven days, we will cure you of this childish desire. Right now you are going to complete the first step in this process and begin your journey to health and wellness. Please standby for your first exercise.

The screen went black and a message scrolled across the screen: *Don't Be a Wannabe.* As the last letters travelled off the screen, a paragraph appeared with the following instructions:

Please rewrite this paragraph one hundred times, in one hundred different ways. Once you have finished this exercise, you will receive your dinner. Please note that if you repeat any combination of three or more words, those words will be deleted, and you will receive an electric shock. You may begin.

The instructions disappeared.

An empty text box materialized. The number one was displayed in large type in the top righthand corner of the box. Polly read the paragraph that she was supposed to rewrite one hundred times. It was seven sentences long and described a pair of pumpkins sitting in a mucky, flooded field.

She clicked on the text box. The cursor blinked at her. She wondered how painful the shock would be and what would happen if she just ignored the exercise and worked on the homework Ms. Whitford had given her.

Polly held the pads of her fingers just above the keys. Ms. Whitford must know where she was. It must have been she who had put the muzzle, mirror, and Scrum food in her suitcase. But what if the doctor found out Scrum was in her room? Would she take him away from her? Polly knew if he was given the opportunity to leave, Scrum would take it, especially if he was tempted with factory-fresh laptops and the promise of flying outside. That would be the end of their relationship and her writing career, for sure.

Polly examined the other girls. They were all about her age, but she did not recognize any faces. She wondered if they had dragons and, if they did, whether their dragons were at the clinic too. Polly placed her fingers on the keyboard and started rewriting the pumpkin paragraph. She might as well play along, for now.

★

Downstairs, in the clinic's warehouse, Scrum was feasting on a delicious assortment of factory-fresh laptops. For the first time since leaving his cave, he had a full stomach. Felix had not stayed long once the pallet was unwrapped. The only thing the dragon had said to him before leaving was, "Eat up, ugly. The doctor's got a little surprise for you."

Scrum had no idea what Felix had meant. He hadn't asked and, for the moment, he didn't care. Being full was making him sleepy. And when he couldn't wolf down another chip or wire, he curled up on the remaining edibles on the pallet. He was content and drifted into a deep sleep, in which he dreamed he was back in his cave.

Scrum didn't hear the intruder, but when he tried to move, he couldn't. He couldn't even wiggle his wing claws, and someone was whispering in his immobilized ear.

"Don't struggle, Scrum. I'm Ms. Whitford, Polly's writing teacher. I'm here to rescue both of you. I need you to stay quiet and be perfectly still, so I can cut these wires."

Laura Michelle Thomas

Scrum whimpered and strained.

"Sh. I put the muzzle on you to keep you quiet, but I didn't tie you up. The nurses did, while you were sleeping. They must have put a sleeping drug in your food. So don't struggle. I'm going to cut the wires, and we are going to find Polly. If you struggle, I might cut you. Do you understand?"

Scrum blinked at Ms. Whitford to show he understood.

Ms. Whitford carefully cut the wires that bound Scrum to the pallet, starting with his tail. The snip of the cutters echoed audibly, so she kept pausing to listen for footsteps and voices.

When Scrum's mid-section was free, he thought about giving Ms. Whitford a good squeeze or a blast of flame as payment for muzzling him, but he didn't. Aside from the delicious meal, Felix had not been kind to him. He also realized it would be impossible to remove the muzzle without Ms. Whitford's help.

★

Upstairs in the dining hall, Polly had stopped typing. She didn't dare touch the keys again because she had just witnessed the girl, who sat directly across the table from her, get shocked sixteen times in a matter of minutes. Before that, the girl on Polly's right had been shocked seven times. Now, both girls had tears streaming down their wet, red cheeks, but they kept typing. Polly stared at her unfinished, second rewrite of the paragraph and tucked her hands under her thighs. She couldn't look at the girls.

A nurse came into the room. Polly looked at her. There was something odd about her. She was clearly wearing a cheap, blonde wig and heavy make-up. She kept her head down and away from Polly, like she was hiding her face. She walked over to the girl who had been shocked sixteen times. Then, tenderly, without interrupting the girl's typing rhythm, the odd-looking nurse dried her cheeks with a pale pink washcloth.

When she was done drying the girl's tears, the nurse looked directly at Polly. Though the face was heavily made-up and the hair wasn't her own, Polly knew it was Ms. Whitford. She wasn't sure what she was supposed to do or how Ms. Whitford was going to get her out.

As if sensing Polly's panic, Ms. Whitford clenched her jaw and shook her head slightly to signal that Polly should remain where she was. There were three distinct pops, and Polly knew the girl beside her had just been shocked again. She watched another nurse, a real nurse, come into the hall to wipe this girl's tears. The girl's teeth chattered, but she didn't stop typing. When Polly looked back across the table, Ms. Whitford was gone.

Polly searched the room. Had Ms. Whitford been caught? She hadn't heard anything. Did she leave because the rescue was too risky?

Suddenly, a wall exploded sending shards and clumps of white-painted drywall onto table. Everyone stopped typing and looked up. It was Scrum and Ms. Whitford.

Polly jumped out of her chair, ran across the hall, and clung to Ms. Whitford's uniform. Nurses were running into the room, an alarm was blaring, and from out of the glass table long wires were snaking around the arms and legs of the girls, tying them up so they could not run away. Dr. Mammozarack's voice could be heard in the hallway. She was shouting orders to seal the building and get the guns.

"Have you ever ridden a dragon, Polly?" asked Ms. Whitford.

Polly shook her head.

"Hop up and hang on."

Scrum crouched down. Polly noticed he had been muzzled and instinctively stroked his long neck before climbing up behind Ms. Whitford. She wrapped her arms tightly around the woman's thick waist.

Ms. Whitford leaned forward. "Fly, Scrum!" she said.

Laura Michelle Thomas

The dragon lurched forward and upward so hard and fast that Polly almost fell off. Before she could adjust her grip, Scrum was airborne and flying in big wide circles around the hall, getting up speed. There were dozens of nurses with guns in the room, all pointed at Scrum, who flew faster and faster with each loop.

"It has been a long time, Masterteller," shouted Dr. Mammozarack.

"What are you up to, Miriam? What is this place?"

Dr. Mammozarack laughed. "Put your guns down. We've got them."

Ms. Whitford squeezed Polly's arms and said, "Hang on tight."

Polly's hair stood straight up as Scrum's wings beat the air in the room into a vortex. Ms. Whitford lay as flat as she could on Scrum's back. Polly did the same. Scrum burst out through a rain of cement into the cool spring evening.

Scrum pumped his wings. "I'm flying! I'm outside!"

Polly was relieved. She loosened her grip on Ms. Whitford's waist and was about to ask where they were going when she noticed Scrum was no longer flying horizontally but was steadily climbing straight up into the darkening sky. Polly could feel herself starting to lose contact with Scrum's scaly back. Scrambling, she lost her grip entirely and started to fall.

The wind rushed by so fast and furiously she couldn't call for help.

She wasn't in the air long before Scrum grabbed her with his tail and put her back down on his back behind Ms. Whitford, who smiled at Polly. "Hold on really tight. We're going to dive."

Polly panted and shook all over, but was able to nod and give Ms. Whitford a slight smile in return.

Scrum had stopped moving and was now hovering midair. Polly's stomach felt as if it was in her chest. Without warning, the dragon tipped headfirst, pointed his muzzled snout downward, and began to dive straight down. The ground came up so fast Polly had to close her eyes to keep from screaming. She did not see that Scrum was heading nose-first at the reflecting pool that she had admired from her room at the clinic.

★

Dr. Mammozarack sneered as she watched the spade of Scrum's white tail slip beneath the dark surface of the reflecting pool. "That was a surprise," she said.

Felix looked up at her. "What did you want with that girl and her skinny dragon? He was as dense as a doorknob, untrainable I'm sure."

The doctor frowned. "I thought they might be useful. The implant still needs work, and I can always use new test subjects. You, of all creatures, should understand that."

Felix rubbed the scar on his forehead. "It's an endless expense, these experiments of yours. Too expensive, if you ask me."

"Are you still pining away for that useless little dragon? The wretched creature died well enough, all in the name of grabbing a literary dragon by its tale and showing it who's boss. Forget about her. Keep your scabby eyes on Yulleg. Trust me. As he gets older, he will be more difficult to control."

Felix scowled at the doctor. "You must go to bed every night worrying about the day Yulleg's success ends and the day he finds out the truth about his parents."

"Ha! Yulleg's parents will never tell him. That boy is a golden goose. Their expensive taste and insatiable greed is insurance enough. They will pay me any amount of money to keep quiet."

"When Yulleg's fame runs out, so will the money. Then they'll tell him the truth."

The doctor snapped at Felix. "This book of yours had better be good. I don't like all this secrecy. If it flops, I will hold you responsible." She snapped her fingers. "I could have you in your urn before sunrise."

Laura Michelle Thomas

Felix laughed. "Wouldn't killing me be like killing the golden goose himself?"

The doctor was about to reply when a nurse approached, carrying a manila envelope.

"What is it?" asked Felix and the doctor together.

"It came from the mansion. The boy told a servant to deliver it to a girl named Polly, but we intercepted it."

Felix snapped the envelope out of the nurse's hands.

Dr. Mammozarack towered over Felix, who only came up to her knees. "That was her, the girl with the white dragon. You must do everything you can to strengthen the bond between yourself and Yulleg. Make sure he does not do anything to jeopardize his new book, or I will not only hold you responsible, I'll put an end to your literary career."

Felix snorted. "You need me and the boy. This is just a crush. Yulleg is not going anywhere."

She smiled viciously. "For your sake, I hope not. There is an empty golden urn out there with your name on it, Felix, and with two little words I can put you in it."

She knelt down, put her hand under Felix's chin, and lifted it so their eyes met. With a vicious smile and a callous glint, she said, "You and your girlfriend could be bookends."

Felix turned away so the doctor could not see his tears.

CHAPTER TEN

The Guild

Polly sat alone at a humble wooden table in a brick-lined alcove, far removed from the hustle and bustle of the great hall of the Guild's subterranean headquarters. Headquarters was accessible only through portals like the reflecting pool outside Dr. Mammozarack's clinic. Over the millennia, the Guild had strategically placed portals in every major city across the globe. The underground network of openings all ended in the massive landing bay, which was one level up from the great hall where Polly sat, thinking about everything except her writing.

Scrum, still muzzled, was sitting across the table from Polly, his snout resting on the rough-hewn wood. He was waiting for Polly to explain her story idea to him, as Ms. Whitford had instructed. The muzzle was not allowed to come off until the exercise was finished. He sighed, and the malodorous breeze lifted Polly's papers slightly, but she didn't notice. She was so distracted by the activity in the great hall, and by thoughts of flying through the dark portals, that she could not focus on her work. She couldn't even figure out which story idea she wanted to work on any more—the circus story or the dragon story. When she tried to think about either one, her imagination went fuzzy, and she had nothing to put into words.

Scrum snorted impatiently, and this time the papers blew off the table and onto the stone floor. Though she saw this, Polly left them where they were and studied the white pencil Ms. Whitford had given her, wondering if it had any surprises in it as well. She turned it around in her fingers. *Scrum Food* it said in dark pink lettering along one side. Polly smiled but didn't feed the pencil to Scrum. She wondered if it had come from the infamous dragon dining hall she had already heard about. Apparently, Scrum wasn't the only dragon with digestive issues, abominable smells, and poor manners.

It had been such a night. After being spit out of a portal and taken down to the living quarters, Polly had slept for quite a while. When she had woken up, Ms. Whitford made her eat in the writers' dining hall, which was located as far away from the dragon dining hall as structurally possible. Over tea, Ms. Whitford had told Polly she was to stay at headquarters until the day her mom expected her home. Then she was to go home and continue with school and her private classes with Ms. Whitford, as if she had enjoyed a pleasant stay at Dr. Mammozarack's clinic. While she was at Guild headquarters, Polly was expected to write and train Scrum, nothing else.

After their talk, Ms. Whitford brought Polly up to the great hall and introduced her to a small group of writers, who all referred to Ms. Whitford as "Masterteller." The team's job was to track the world's literary dragon population on huge screens that towered far above their heads. Polly was amazed at the number of white dots covering every part of the map. Against the black screen, Polly thought they looked like a clear night sky loaded with stars.

After a brief tour of the great hall, Ms. Whitford, the Masterteller, had set Polly up at the wooden table in the quiet alcove and left her alone to work on her story.

Scrum huffed again.

Polly looked at him. "Okay. Okay. I know you want that thing off. But I can't. Writing just seems so boring now compared to all this." She pointed the white pencil at the lively, cavernous space filled with a strange mixture of ancient and modern equipment, leather-bound books, and writers.

Ms. Whitford came over and scooped the papers up off the floor. "Haven't you started yet?"

Polly shrugged. "Scrum thinks my ideas are boring."

Ms. Whitford said nothing and cupped a hand to her ear. "I don't hear Scrum saying anything right now. Do you?"

"Well, not right now, but at the clinic he said—"

"Nothing. He said nothing you need to hear right now during this delicate and highly creative stage of the writing process." Ms. Whitford pulled up a chair and sat down. "He shouldn't be saying anything at all until you have written your entire lump of clay. That's when he will be extremely useful, but not before. Dragons and first draft writing don't mix."

Scrum furrowed his forehead and snorted with displeasure.

"Either of your ideas will work just fine as a two-thousand word short story, as long as you focus on one episode and go deeply into it. Create one main character who has one small problem. I don't want you writing a plot summary, which is what can happen if you try to cram a novel-sized idea into a short story." Ms. Whitford put the papers in front of Polly.

"The truth is what you write about doesn't matter. If you want to be a writer, it's not what you write about, it's how well you write it that matters—execution matters more than your subject. And as for this one," she nodded in Scrum's direction, "he doesn't get a say in the idea stage of the writing process, not even in the research or focusing stages, or even in the drafting stage, which we haven't talked about yet. He gets his turn later, and his input will be extremely valuable—better than gold. But if you let him boss you around in the early stages of the

Laura Michelle Thomas

writing process, you'll never finish a piece of writing, period. So look your dragon in the eyes and tell him which story idea you are going to work on. Keep your explanation short and sweet, and then write your three paragraphs on plot, character, and setting."

A bunch of writers came into the hall. It looked to Polly like they were gathering for a meeting. "Is the doctor going to attack us or something? Is there going to be a fight between her and the Guild?"

Ms. Whitford's face reddened, and her lips tightened. "I hope not. But we are going to decide if we need to stop production of Yulleg's book. I hope we don't, but if we do, we will attempt to do it peacefully. There is an ancient saying in the Guild—writers are not fighters—at least not with weapons. The last thing anyone here can do is fire a weapon. Words are a different story. They can be deadly, as you know."

Polly nodded. She had not forgotten that with a single sentence she could kill Scrum. "Is there anything I can do?"

Ms. Whitford smiled at Polly and stood up. She pointed at the sheets of paper on the table. "Keep up with your exercises, do what I say, and keep training Scrum to be your ally, not your enemy. You will need him once you make your lump of clay. But first, you have to teach him how to let you write that lump of clay."

Polly nodded. "That's my first draft, right?"

"I'll tell you what, Polly. Let's speed things up a bit. You still have to do your exercise, but, if you like, you may take the muzzle off Scrum at any time. He is your dragon after all. You are his writer, not I."

"Thank you, Ms. Whitford."

Ms. Whitford was about to tell Polly she could call her Masterteller, but she stopped herself. Only fully-trained writers, with fully-trained dragons, were allowed to call her by that name. As passionate as the girl might be, she still had a long way to go before she could be officially inducted into the Writers' Guild and the responsibilities that came with it. This made her think of the boy, Yulleg, who had been left to his own devices for too long.

"Find me when you are finished, Polly, and I will teach you about focusing," said Ms. Whitford.

Polly didn't want Ms. Whitford to leave. "What's focusing?"

Scrum let out a whine, picked up his chin, and thumped it down noisily on the table.

Ms. Whitford ignored Scrum and sat down. "I'll make this quick. Once you have an idea and have done some research and some writing to thicken up and explore your story, what should you do next?"

"Write the whole story?" shrugged Polly.

"Not quite. Before you dive into the manuscript, I would suggest you do something which is extremely important and will save you buckets of time in the end: focusing your story."

Polly thought back to English class. "Like a thesis statement?"

"Sort of, but thesis statements are for essays and articles, the non-fiction genres. Let me explain. Can you put the whole universe, every single idea in your head, into one story?"

"No way. That's impossible. The story would be thousands of pages long!"

"Right, so you have to accept that this is only one of the many stories you will write during your career. The more focused you can make each story you write, the better unity you will have, and the secret to unity is focusing your idea around two things: a central theme and a working title."

Polly looked at Scrum and felt kind of sorry for him. She tried to speed things up so she could take his muzzle off. "Why a 'working' title?" she asked Ms. Whitford. "What does that mean?"

"'Working' means it works for now, but you might come up with a better title later once you've finished your lump of clay. It's really important that you try to summarize your story with your title as early as possible.

It doesn't have to be perfect, but it does need to fit your story—not any old story, this story, the one you are writing now. It will serve as a sieve for all your ideas, as will your theme statement. Do you know what a sieve is, Polly?"

"Yeah, my mom has one. You push soft foods or flour through the metal mesh; and the large bits and pieces that don't fit, the ones you don't want, get caught and don't end up in your recipe."

"That's what your working title and your theme statement will do for your story, Polly."

"I don't get what you mean by theme statement."

Scrum rolled his eyes.

Polly caught this and quickly changed her mind about taking the muzzle off.

"A theme statement is a one-sentence summary of your story's heart or main topic like, 'this is a story about betrayal,' or 'this is a story about belonging.' The theme is just the big human conundrum your story wrestles with. As human beings, we only have so many problems. Your story will fit one of them somehow. And the more aware you are of your theme, the better your story will be. You've been studying theme in English class for years from a reader's perspective, now you get to think about it from a writer's point of view."

Polly's head was spinning.

Just then, a man respectfully approached and handed Ms. Whitford a manila envelope. It had Polly's name handwritten on it in thick black marker in tall, swooping loops. Underneath her name there was a signature that Polly could not make out from where she sat.

"This just came, Masterteller. It's addressed to Polly."

"Have it fingerprinted and scanned, and let me know what you find."

"Yes, Masterteller." The man nodded and walked away, briskly.

Ms. Whitford stood up, frowning. "Don't worry about the envelope. Choose your story; do your character, plot, and setting paragraphs; and then I'll give you a worksheet that will help you focus your story."

When Ms. Whitford was gone, Polly took the muzzle off Scrum. He yawned and stretched his jaw.

"That's a good dragon," said Polly as she reached out and scratched his chin for the first time. Having Scrum suddenly felt like having a big, ugly pet. Maybe, just maybe, she could get used to him. As Polly scratched, she could feel Scrum relaxing into her fingers. He lifted his chin higher and started to make a deep, vibrating noise that reminded Polly of a cat's purr, only it was more musical.

"Ms. Whitford says it doesn't matter what I write about, as long as I write it well. So I have a new idea for a story—actually it's an old idea. I've never told you about it. Anyway, it's about a girl who finds a silver bullet that turns her into a creature called a vamperwolf. That's a half werewolf, half vampire creature."

Scrum was about to say something, when Polly sensed the oncoming criticisms and stopped scratching. "I don't care what you think right now. Ms. Whitford says writers don't need their dragons until they have written the first draft of their story. So all you get to do is listen and nod and tell me how good my story idea is and that I'm a good writer."

Scrum lifted his chin, urging Polly to keep scratching.

"Good. I think we do have an understanding, then." She pulled her hand away and picked up the white pencil. "There will be more of that later, Scrum. Why don't you go to the famous dragon dining hall and get something to eat?"

Scrum's eyes lit up.

"I still wish you hadn't eaten my laptop. I type much faster than I can write with a pencil. Is there any way you can give it back to me? Are you sure it's not sitting inside you somewhere?"

"I'm sure it's...ah...gone." Scrum's white face flushed with dark pink splotches.

Laura Michelle Thomas

"What if I get another laptop some day? Will you try to eat that one, too?"

Scrum looked very serious and said matter-of-factly, "Definitely. Laptops are delicious."

Polly threw her hands up in the air. "How did you get a taste for that stuff? Before we...ah...met...you were in a cave, by yourself. So who fed you laptops in there?"

The bridge of Scrum's nose wrinkled as he concentrated. "Once every day, a hole opened in the wall of my cave, and a big juicy pile of laptops tumbled in. There was nothing else to eat, so that's what I ate. I never thought about it until the day you tried to feed me pencils. Those are a good snack, but they don't fill me up, not even a little bit."

"You are so strange. I don't know how your body can digest all that stuff. Is that what every dragon eats?"

Scrum went cross-eyed as he tried to remember what he knew about dragon diets. "I think so, but I've never actually talked to another dragon, except Felix, and we didn't talk about that, so I don't know for sure."

"Go get something to eat. I'm going to write."

Scrum hesitated.

"What's wrong?" asked Polly.

"They are all Guild dragons. What if they don't like me, or they think I'm ugly or weird, or they pick on me because I'm new?"

"If you're hungry, you have to eat, right?"

Scrum's stomach gurgled loudly.

"You had better go before you starve to death."

Scrum stood up but didn't move.

"You'll be fine. And just think, it's a dragon dining hall. The food is bound to be delicious. The people food sure was."

Scrum resigned himself and left.

Polly watched him go, then she picked up her pencil and thought about her story, but it was hard to get her mind off the mysterious envelope. What was it about? No one knew where she was, not even her mom. Polly twirled the pencil on its tip and watched the grey dots it left on the blank sheet of paper.

CHAPTER ELEVEN

Yulleg

Yulleg was bored. He was bored of school, bored of living in a mansion, extremely bored of writing, and, at the moment, sick and tired of listening to Felix yammer about *Dragon by a Tale*. The dwarfish dragon was on pins and needles waiting for the book to be published and equally on pins and needles about keeping the story a secret from Dr. Mammozarack. But Yulleg no longer cared about writing, about this particular book, or even about Felix's tiny broken heart. He was detached, indifferent to all of it. There was no challenge left, nothing in it for him. It stung that he had squandered his childhood tapping away on a computer. It all seemed terribly mundane now and a huge waste of time. He was done with book signings and author interviews. Everything in his life connected to writing and publishing bored him, which meant just about everything in his life bored him, except one thing. There was a girl, and she was intriguing, riveting, gripping, interesting, and not boring at all. And Yulleg had done something bold. He had sent her a gift.

Felix swatted Yulleg's shin. "Are you listening to me, boy?"

"Ouch!" Yulleg glared at his dragon. For more than a decade he had done everything Felix had asked him to do. He wrote. Felix edited. He became famous. And during the last two years, he had done everything he had been asked to do for the new book. He had kept the story a secret from Dr. Mammozarack and had successfully negotiated with the publishing company—Mightright out of Mongolia—to keep the story hidden from the public until its release date. Even though this latest book was probably going to be dubbed his masterpiece, Yulleg was done with it all. He had given a great deal to Felix, and the world's readers, but his time had come. He was ready and longing to create a new chapter in his life that had nothing do to with his past.

Felix pointed at him with a scabby claw. "You've got it pretty good compared to other kids your age. They would kill for your fame and fortune. Just look at this place. You've got a screen in every room, each one bigger than the next. Your parents are always off traveling the world leaving you with cute nannies, who cater to your every whim. Well, guess what, boy? I can take it all away with a snap of my fingers."

"You don't have fingers," yawned Yulleg. "And you need me. I'm the celebrity author, not you. It's my face on the inside cover of those books, not yours. I'm the one who has to be on tour signing autographs when the next book comes out."

"You will finish what we have started." Felix hiked himself up onto Yulleg's lap. "Her story must be told!" he shrieked. Then he paused and softened his voice. "You know how much this means to me."

Yulleg kicked his knees and tried to jostle the dragon off his lap, but Felix snarled and hung on to Yulleg's t-shirt. "I won't. I don't care about your great lost love or book sales. Launch it without me. I'm going to find—never mind. Just know that I'm not writing another word or signing another autograph."

"You will do what you are told or—"

"Or what?"

Felix smiled and tightened his grip on Yulleg's t-shirt. "Or I will do something terrible to Polly."

Laura Michelle Thomas

Yulleg was caught off guard. He had not told a soul about Polly. "I don't know who you are talking about. I've never met a Polly, except for some dumb girl in my English class. But she's not my type."

"I have proof to the contrary."

Yulleg grabbed Felix with both hands and tried to pull him off. "Let go of me! I don't care about anyone named Polly."

Felix dug his claws in deeper.

Yulleg pulled harder.

Felix held on. "Well, that's interesting, because we intercepted the person you sent to deliver—" Just then Yulleg's t-shirt ripped. Felix lost his grip and tumbled backwards onto the plush carpet.

"This!" said Felix, holing up a leather necklace. Dangling from it was the most skillful carving Yulleg had ever done—a red-stained, cedar dragon with out-stretched wings. The wings reached out sideways from the dragon's forward-facing, muscular body. Its scaly, spiny neck curved in the opposite direction from its curled tail, which looped back on itself in a figure-eight and disappeared behind one of its wings. The head was shown in profile with the jaws open and teeth bared. It hung on a simple leather thong, ready to speak or to breathe fire, or perhaps both in a single breath.

"Give me that carving, Felix. It's not yours."

"So you do like her."

Yulleg tried to seem calm and unaffected by the threat. "I'm fifteen. I think all the girls are pretty. I'm going to make one for every girl in my English class. I just happened to make one for her first. It was random. The envelope could have been addressed to any of them."

Felix glared at him. "Then you won't mind if I send her to the doctor?"

Yulleg held his face still for a moment then forced it to break into a carefree smile. "Why would you risk hurting one of our number one fans?"

"Oh, I don't think we have to worry about that!"

"What do you mean by that?"

Felix shrugged innocently. "Let's just say I don't think your girlfriend is going to be a Yulleg Snoblivski fan any longer."

"What have you done?"

"Oh, nothing at all, yet. It all depends on you." The dragon didn't blink. "So, will you be a good boy and do as you are told?"

Yulleg couldn't tell if Felix was telling the truth or not. He sighed. "Only if you swear on your love for Quill not to send her to Mammozarack."

Felix raised a claw in the air. "I swear on my beloved's silver urn she will not be harmed."

Yulleg ground his molars together. "Deal. Now, get out of my room. I'm extremely bored with all this."

Felix tossed the necklace to Yulleg and turned to leave. He raised his voice and called to someone who was waiting outside the door. "You can pretty him up for the photo shoot now, Ted."

A cheerless man strode into the room. Yulleg nodded at him but didn't say hello. Ted returned the greeting.

Felix continued giving orders as he walked out the door. "Then bring him down to the studio. Be quick about it. I need the book cover finalized tonight."

"You heard him, kid. Let's get you cleaned up."

"I'm not cooperating."

Ted shook his head. "You don't have a choice at the moment. None of us do. So, let's just get it over with. You'd better start by putting on a different shirt. It looks like you've been attacked by a gang of wild cats." He chuckled.

Yulleg almost smiled. "Something like that, but I'm not changing my shirt."

Ted's smile disappeared. He came over to where Yulleg lounged on a plush leather sofa, pulled him up by the arms, and dragged him to the lavish master bathroom.

Laura Michelle Thomas

Ted pushed Yulleg roughly up to the sink and turned on the cold water. He thrust a washcloth at Yulleg. "Wash up and I'll get you a shirt."

Yulleg snatched the cloth out of Ted's hands. "You can go now," he ordered. "I can wash my own face and get my own shirt."

Ted shook his head. "Sorry, kid. I don't believe you will."

Yulleg glared at the man he had come to think of as a father. "Then Felix can wait all night."

Ted snatched the washcloth out of Yulleg's hands and ran it under frigid water. He wrung it out, opened it up, and put in on Yulleg's face. Yulleg struggled and tried to push it away, but Ted held the cloth tightly. "This isn't a game, kid. There is a lot of money, a lot of high lifestyle, riding on your success. Look at this place. Do you think your parents want to come home and find a foreclosure sign on the front lawn?" He let go of the washcloth.

Yulleg's cheeks were red, and he threw the cloth in the sink. "What about what I want? I'm getting sick and tired of being everyone's gravy train. How much money have you been making editing my books these last two years, Ted? What about for your work on *Dragon by a Tale*? How much?"

Ted's jaws tightened. "Just get ready for your photo shoot, kid. We don't have time to argue. Felix seems more riled up than usual. What's the story with that envelope business?"

"I made that for a girl." Yulleg pointed at the counter where he had placed the necklace.

Ted relaxed and smiled. "Oh yeah, what girl?"

"This girl in my English class. Her name's Polly. I'm going to ask her out next week when all this book hullabaloo is over."

"Hey. That's my kid's name." Ted slapped Yulleg on the back. "What makes your Polly so special? You've got girls camped out on the sidewalk almost every weekend. Is she one of those?"

"No. I don't even think she's into my books all that much. She's really quiet in English. She's never asked me for an autograph. I like that. And she's quirky, her family too. Her friend told me her dad is a tractor salesman. I had no idea that was even a job." Yulleg laughed.

Ted's smile disappeared. "That's my Polly!"

"She's your daughter? Really?" Yulleg's cheeks went a deeper shade of red. "Is that why she was at Mammozarack's office the other day? No wonder Felix was so cocky. They know who she is. They might have her already. They know she's your kid, right?"

A tremor ran through Ted's body. "You saw Polly at Miriam's office?"

Yulleg nodded. "I stopped by to sign a bunch of first editions. I literally bumped into Polly in the waiting room. I think I might have cut her or her purse or something, accidentally. She had just come out of Mammozarack's office."

Ted lowered his voice. "Cut her? What? You better not have. I don't want my daughter anywhere near that woman. I never thought—I've been so busy getting to know you that..." Ted shook his head. "What have I done?"

"Why get to know me? What are you talking about?"

"Your father was my best friend."

"What do you mean was? I thought you just met him for the first time when you came to work with us."

"Not him, your real father. His name was Johan. Our dragons are...were...are twins."

"Hold on a second. My dad is on a Mediterranean cruise with my mom right now. He's not dead. And he definitely doesn't have a literary dragon that looks like Xelif. He's not a writer; he's an executive at a major car company."

Ted put down the lid on the toilet seat. "You'd better sit down, kid."

Yulleg crossed his arms and leaned against the sink. "I'm fine right here, thanks."

"Suit yourself." Ted sat down on the toilet. "Here's the deal. The people you think are your real parents, aren't. They adopted you a day or so after you were born. I'm sorry no one has told you the truth, but I've got to imagine it's got a lot to do with all the money riding on your success." He sighed.

"I didn't even know Johan had a son until I saw you and Felix at that bookstore in New York two years ago. I never would have agreed to come on as proofreader if it hadn't been for meeting you and finding out who you were. My dragon, Xelif, is Felix's twin brother. I know they don't look anything alike anymore, but they are. It's how I figured out you're Johan's kid. Felix was your father's dragon. He should have died when your father died, but he didn't. Then he formed a bond with you that I cannot explain. I don't even know how Felix survived. None of this should have happened. Felix should have died when your father—"

Yulleg stared at him with wide, disbelieving eyes and a smirk on his face. "If you're telling the truth, then who's my mother?"

"You're not going to want to hear this," sighed Ted.

"Try me," said Yulleg.

"I don't know, for certain, who your mother is, though I can make a pretty good guess based on your age and what your father was up to in those days. I've always suspected she had something to do with your father's death—his murder, maybe—but the Guild wouldn't listen to me. Now she's got Polly involved and—"

"No way!" Yulleg shook his head vigorously. "Miriam Mammozarack—that bughouse doctor—are you saying she's my real mother, and Felix, who looks nothing like Xelif, is his twin brother and was my father's dragon? Ha! I think you have been writing fiction too long old man. No one has ever told me I was adopted. There is no way she is my mother. And Felix and Xelif are not twins. Impossible! You're lying. Get out of here. I'm leaving. I'm leaving all of this."

Ted stood up. "I don't really care what you believe because, right now, I've got to make sure Polly is okay. That's all that matters. When I realized who you were...I never should have let myself get so distracted from my responsibilities..." Ted looked straight at Yulleg. "I don't care what you do with this information, kid. I know what your father would have wanted you to do, but you're almost a man. You need to be able to live with whatever choice you make. As for me, I'm going to Guild headquarters. They might know where Polly is."

"Guild? Headquarters? Oh, this makes your story so much more believable. How dumb do you think I am?"

"Like it or not, kid, I'm telling you the truth. I used to belong to a worldwide Writers' Guild. They help kids like you learn to train their dragons. The Guild has two mottos: writers are not fighters, and the world needs stories."

"Cheesy mottos. But I'm not buying any of it. I think writing fiction has made you go insane."

"Believe what you want. I'm leaving. I can't let anything happen to Polly." Ted turned to leave.

"Wait," said Yulleg.

Ted turned around. "What? You believe me all of a sudden?"

"No. I still think you've written one too many stories, but I want out. Take me to your mysterious Guild."

"I don't think so, kid." Ted rubbed his stubbled chin. "I think you'd better stay here at the mansion. You're not ready to make it out there in real world—you know the one without limos, servants, and a titanium credit card."

On the inside Yulleg exploded, but he managed to keep his voice calm. "I have done enough for these people. I want out. I don't care if I ever see Felix again. As for the crazy doctor...listen, I'm going with you. So where is this Guild and how do we get there?"

Ted nodded. "It's closer than you think." He walked over to one of the tall bathroom windows and looked

Laura Michelle Thomas

down at the elaborate hedgerows surrounding the garden.

Yulleg followed him to the window. "Guild head-quarters is in the garden?"

"No. There's a reflecting pool in the middle of those shrubs. You can't see it from the house. It's a gateway to an underground network of tunnels, a portal they call it."

"I can't swim," Yulleg said, feebly.

"Don't worry, kid. You won't even get wet." Yulleg looked at the older man quizzically. Ted grinned. "Have you ever ridden a dragon?"

"Um, have you seen Felix?"

"Right. Well, there's a first time for everything."

Yulleg grabbed the dragon pendant off the counter and followed Ted out onto the marble sundeck and down a sweeping stairway to the garden. He chased Ted through the hedgerows, ducking when Ted ducked, creeping forward when Ted crept, freezing when Ted froze. Yulleg's guts were in knots by the time they reached the reflecting pool. It looked bigger and deeper up close than it had from above, and he was extremely anxious about going in the water.

"Good. No guards," said Ted. He whistled softly.

The hedges pitched and heaved as a powerful, broad-chested dragon came crashing out. Without instruction, Xelif bowed his head and lowered his sleek, red-scaled back.

"In the garden!" Felix shouted from the sundeck. "Get Yulleg! Don't let him go!" An alarm sounded and a gun fired once, twice...

"Get on, and hang on tight, kid!"

Yulleg scrambled onto Xelif's back and wrapped his arms around Ted's waist.

"Ready, kid?"

Yulleg nodded.

"Fly, Xelif!"

The dragon shot straight up into the overcast sky. Yulleg lurched and tightened his hold on Ted.

Just when Yulleg thought he couldn't hold on any longer, Xelif stopped flying straight upward and hovered for a moment in midair. Yulleg barely caught his breath before the dragon tipped his entire body, from nose to tail, directly at the ground and began to dive.

The reflecting pool rushed up at them. "We're going to die!" shouted Yulleg. The force of the wind pummeled his cheeks, making the flesh flap wildly.

Ted looked over his shoulder with a smile. "Nope. If we're going to die, it'll be when I show up at Guild headquarters without an invitation."

★

Moments after Xelif touched down on the ancient stone floor of the landing bay at Guild headquarters, Ted and Yulleg were handcuffed.

"It's nice to be back," Ted told the young men who handcuffed them. "Are you taking us to the Masterteller? Hope she's well. I'm looking forward to getting reacquainted with the old place." He smiled cordially.

Yulleg was speechless from his first flight through a portal, the imposing structure of the landing bay, and the fact that Ted seemed to be telling the truth and what that meant about his family. Despite the shock, he did his best to play along and pretend they were just dropping by to visit old friends.

The guards, who were not much older than Yulleg, glanced at each other but didn't answer. They had been given strict instructions not to engage the prisoners in conversation.

Laura Michelle Thomas

CHAPTER TWELVE

Lumps Of Clay

Polly was reeling from the news. "Kill me, but why would Yulleg Snoblivski want to kill me?" She gaped at the steel containment box, its thick metal sides disfigured by the blast.

Ms. Whitford wrapped her arm protectively around Polly's shoulders and hugged her close. "I don't think it was Yulleg. He probably had no idea there was a bomb in that envelope. But listen, I don't want you to worry about any of this. The bomb was probably just a warning that the Guild should mind its own business. Somebody wants to keep the contents of *Dragon by a Tale* a secret. This isn't the first time rogue writers have asked us to keep our noses of their work, and it won't be the last. But it's our job to make sure the world is a friendly place for all writers, not just a chosen few."

A woman approached Ms. Whitford. "The prisoners are ready for questioning, Masterteller."

"Prisoners?" Polly shook Ms. Whitford's arm loose and turned to look at her.

"Yulleg and your father are downstairs."

"My dad? He's here? How? He's not a writer. He sells combines and seeders and cultivators and disk mowers and augers and gravity wagons and—"

Ms. Whitford stopped Polly with a raised eyebrow.

Polly shrugged. "You can't blame me for wanting to know what my dad does for work."

"Polly, I don't know how to say this, but your father is not a tractor salesman."

Polly frowned, and her cheeks went red. She was furious at the thought she had been lied to. "Then what is he, and why has he been away most of my life?"

Ms. Whitford looked directly at Polly. "He's a writer."

"A writer? Like with a literary dragon and everything and all this?" Polly spread her arms wide as if to take in the entire great hall, including the massive, round table where the Guild held its meetings.

Ms. Whitford's face softened, and her eyes moistened slightly. She cleared her throat. "An excellent one, who has been published in dozens of countries."

Polly put her hands on her hips. "I don't believe it. If that's true, why haven't I ever heard of him?"

"You should probably ask him to explain. From my point of view, he loves the money but despises fame, so he writes under a pseudonym, several pseudonyms actually. His work goes under at least two dozen different pen names."

"I don't get it."

"Your father doesn't like to draw attention to himself, and he seems to enjoy the freedom of writing pieces that are worshipped in some markets and despised in others. The pseudonyms allow him flexibility. As long as I have known him, he has been a man who values freedom and independence above all else. He has never been a team player, more of a writer-for-hire, a rogue through and through. Any story, any time, as long as the pay is good."

"Does my mom know?"

Ms. Whitford shook her head. "I don't believe so. We don't recommend writers marry outside the Guild. He estranged himself from the Guild right after Johan's death. He was angry, and I imagine he still is. I'm sure the only reason he's here is to make sure you're okay."

"Can I see him?"

"I haven't decided yet. In the meantime, I would like you to write your lump of clay. Then I can give you this." She pulled the red plastic egg out of her pocket and held it out for Polly to see. Then she nodded in the direction of Polly's alcove.

"Fine," Polly huffed as she turned away from Ms. Whitford. She stared up at the massive computer screens as she walked across the hall to her work table. A new light blinked on in South Africa. It was neat to see a new literary dragon being born, but at the same time Polly didn't like the idea of there being yet another blossoming young writer in the world to compete with. She suddenly wished she was the only one, then she would definitely be able to get her work published.

Scrum was curled up around the thick tables legs, snoring. When Polly sat down, he opened his eyes but didn't get up. His stomach growled loudly.

"How can you be hungry again?"

Scrum blinked rapidly, as if he didn't understand the question.

"Go down to the dragon dining hall, then."

"Can't you go down there and bring me some food?"

"I could, but why don't you want to go down there?"

Scrum licked his lips with his pink tongue. "Because... because...because..."

"Because? C'mon, Scrum. What's wrong?"

"Because...they laughed at me and said I was weird."

Polly had to bite her lip to stifle a laugh. "You are weird! Haven't you seen yourself? You look more like a snake than a dragon, your skin is a sickly shade of white, your nostrils are miles too wide for your face, and you stink. If they make dragon deodorant here, you should get some."

Scrum furrowed his brows and narrowed his eyes. "I could singe all your hair off with one good burp. Then you'd see what it's like to be called weird."

Polly leaned across the table and grabbed Scrum by the scruff of his hairy chin. "And I could kill you with one sentence."

"You could?"

"I can, but I wouldn't because, as weird as you are, you are a pretty good dragon for a writer to have."

"A wannabe writer," corrected Scrum.

Polly released his beard and deflated back across the table into her chair. "Once I finish this story, and it is ready to send to a publisher, they will probably ask me—beg me—to join the Guild."

Scrum stretched his jaws. "I don't think a single short story gets you into the Guild. And even if it does, you have to finish it first, which seems to be highly problematic for you."

Scrum had spoken to the nub of it. Optimistic as she had been when she decided to work on her vamperwolf story, it was a whole different thing to actually sit down and write an entire first draft with a beginning, middle, and end. What if she got stuck? What if the story got away from her? What if it really would be better as a novel? What if it was just like all those other stories she had abandoned? She knew Ms. Whitford only wanted a lump of clay—a really rough draft with spelling mistakes and everything—but the thing Polly was most frightened of was the ending. What if she couldn't think of one?

"I need to see Ms. Whitford, right away."

"But I'm hungry."

"You have a choice, Scrum. You accept you're weird and go eat with the other dragons or you starve. I don't care what you do. I have to find Ms. Whitford." Polly got up and hurried across to where the writers sat, monitoring the screens.

"But you're supposed to write your story!" called Scrum.

Polly ignored him. There was no way she was going to be able to write a whole story, and she knew it. She just hoped Ms. Whitford would have a way to fix it.

Polly soon learned Ms. Whitford had given strict instructions that she was not to be disturbed. Polly begged to be allowed to see her and was, after much

Laura Michelle Thomas

pleading, escorted to a stone elevator by an exasperated female writer. She stepped inside and pulled Polly in behind her. The box was just big enough for the two of them. The writer pulled a lever, and they started going down, slowly.

When the stone elevator finally stopped, the doors opened, revealing an unlit hallway. "Put these glasses on," said the writer, "and follow the voices." Polly took the glasses and put them on. They brightened the hallway just enough to allow her to see a row of doors lining one side. Then the elevator doors crunched shut, leaving Polly alone in the dark.

She put one hand on the wall and followed the voices. Sound travelled extremely well in the hallway so Polly found herself making several turns before she came to an open door.

"Come in, Polly," said Ms. Whitford, curtly.

"Polly, my girl, is that you?"

Polly's throat thickened, and she didn't want to say anything. She had mixed emotions about seeing her dad. He was sitting in a large chair in the middle of the spacious room, and though she couldn't be certain, it looked as if he was being held down by thick straps across his thighs and chest. She knew Ms. Whitford probably wasn't hurting him, but a deep, dark, nasty sliver of Polly's heart wanted him to be punished severely for lying to her. She spoke only to Ms. Whitford. "I need help."

"Hallway. Now."

"I can help her, Patti. We're just about done, right? Let me up. I want to give my girl a hug." Ted's eyes were monstrously wide from trying to see in the dark. He wasn't wearing the special glasses, but Ms. Whitford was. "Patti! Patti!" he called.

Ms. Whitford left the door partway open and ushered Polly a few steps away from it.

"Why is it so dark down here?" Polly whispered.

Polly's dad continued pleading, calling out for her.

Ms. Whitford answered so loudly, she was almost yelling. "You see, Polly, darkness calms the overly creative mind. Sometimes, extraordinary calmness is needed in order to extract the truth from those who spend their lives writing highly believable fiction. Sometimes the habit of lying in fiction spills over into the real world, and extreme measures must be taken to extract the truth from such a vivid imagination. I want to know that whatever he tells me about Yulleg's book is the truth." Ms. Whitford paused.

Polly's dad had gone silent.

She lowered her voice. "Why did you come down here, Polly? Is there an emergency? Did something happen to Scrum?"

"No...I...well...maybe...it's not an emergency really... I..." Polly suddenly felt pathetic about needing help. What was wrong with her that she couldn't just sit down and whip off a first draft of a short story? Ms. Whitford did not expect a perfectly polished manuscript with every punctuation mark in its proper place. Polly felt ashamed she couldn't just do it on her own.

Ms. Whitford sighed. Polly's expression told her exactly what was wrong, and she felt guilty. It was her fault. The girl still wasn't ready, nor should she be at this stage of her career. Gently, she turned Polly around and started walking her back to the elevator.

"With everything going on, I haven't given you enough instruction. You have Scrum well enough in hand, and you seem to understand he is not to interfere in the writing process at this early stage."

Polly nodded. "I think Scrum and I are doing okay. We don't always get along perfectly—"

"And that's completely normal," interrupted Ms. Whitford. "Every partnership between dragon and writer is unique. There is no one-size-fits-all solution when it comes to nurturing the dragon-writer bond. I fear I have missed a step or two and sent you straight into writing your lump of clay without helping you prepare. You have chosen your story idea, right?"

"Yes, but it's not one of the ideas I thought of at your house. Is that okay?"

"Of course! Any story idea will work. Have you written out your three paragraphs on character, plot, and setting yet?"

"No." Polly was embarrassed to admit it.

"Oh dear! This is worse than I thought. Before you can really sit down and write the first draft of your story with confidence, you need to do a bit more research and focusing."

Ms. Whitford continued as they walked through the dark passageway. "Before you go upstairs and catch up, I need you to spend some time imagining the key scenes in your story. It will help a great deal. After you explore and develop those scenes, I would like you to think of a working title and a theme statement, and write those three paragraphs I asked you to on plot, setting, and main character. Then you will be ready to write your first draft."

Ms. Whitford stopped walking. They were back at the elevator.

"But how?"

"Do you see the bench over there?"

"No."

"Just down there, in that alcove." Ms. Whitford turned Polly so she could see a low stone bench set in a shallow alcove off the hallway. It was covered with a thick, dark upholstery.

"Go and lie down on your back and remove your glasses. Once settled, you will hear a bell ring three times. When you hear the bell, I want you to begin imagining the opening scene of your story. Let your mind dive into the scene. Say yes to everything that comes to you. Scrum is not here, so you have no reason to hold back or second-guess what your imagination spontaneously creates. Let it flow. Let it make you laugh out loud or cry.

"When you hear the bell again, switch your imagination to your climax and explore that scene with rich colour and vivid sensory detail. After a while, you will hear the bell again, and you will switch to the last scene of your story, the very end, and do the same thing until the bell rings three times. Do you understand?"

Polly shrugged. "Will lying down here in the dark by myself really help me write my first draft?"

"Yes. And you're not alone. Your father and I are just down the hall. We will be here for a while still, I imagine."

"Are you hurting him?"

"No. Of course not. We are just getting reacquainted. Don't let the darkness frighten you. It can be soothing. Go on, Polly. Lie down and get started on your visualizations. You have a story inside you that needs some time and space to come out. I will see you soon." Ms. Whitford turned to go.

"Do I do any writing after this?"

"Of course. You have a lot of writing to do! Funny how it is with writers, always more writing to do." Ms. Whitford stopped and turned around. "Polly..."

"Yes, Ms. Whitford."

"Your father will be fine. Don't let what's going on around you stop you from writing. It's your job."

Polly went over to the alcove, took off the glasses, and lay down on the plush bench in complete darkness. Ms. Whitford's footsteps receded down the hallway, and a bell rang three times signaling Polly was to begin imagining the opening scene of her story.

★

Polly had enjoyed being in the dark and was able to concentrate on her scenes for a while, but when the bell had rung to signal that she should switch from visualizing the climax to visualizing the last scene, she couldn't concentrate any more. Thoughts about her dad being a writer kept breaking the surface of her inner movie screen, bursting up like inky bubbles that blacked out the images. Before the final bell had rung, Polly had given up and was in the elevator, on her way up to find Scrum.

Polly looked for him in the great hall, but he wasn't there. No one had seen him since she'd gone down to the dark floor. Then, one of the writers told her several dragons were on their way from the dragon dining hall to the landing bay, preparing for a mission. The woman suggested to Polly that Scrum—being a young, unschooled dragon—might be thinking he could go along with them.

"Mission? Where?" Polly asked.

"Mightright Publishing Company's corporate head-quarters in the Altai Mountains in southwestern Mongolia," said Ms. Whitford, coming up beside Polly. "We are sending out a team to stop the production of *Dragon by a Tale*. According to your father and Yulleg, it contains a rather detailed history of Guild activities. I cannot allow it to go public unless I'm sure there are enough layers of fiction between us and the world. I understand that Felix is in a rush to get it printed before Miriam finds out it's about her dragon, Quill, and Miriam's ill treatment of the poor creature. We think they are going to try and start the print run tonight. We need to get there before they start the press."

"We have time," said Ted, walking up to where Polly and Ms. Whitford were standing behind the line of manned computers in front of the big screens. "They don't have Yulleg's new photo for the cover, and I haven't finished proofing the galleys. I've still got three chapters to go. They might delay the run for a few days."

Polly turned to face him. "Dad! Why didn't you tell me you're a writer?"

Her dad shrugged and, for a moment, looked younger than Yulleg, who had just sauntered up beside him.

Polly glared at them both. And when Yulleg grinned at her, she punched him in the stomach.

Yulleg doubled over. "What's that for?"

"Nearly stabbing me and almost blowing me up!"

Polly's dad smirked and winked at Ms. Whitford. "It must be love."

Ms. Whitford narrowed her eyes. "Do you want a punch in the gut too, Ted?"

"Now, Patti, that's—"

Ms. Whitford shook her index finger at Ted. Polly had never seen her so upset. "Don't you ever call me by my first name, not here, not now, not ever!"

"Yes, Masterteller!" Ted gave her a mock salute.

Ms. Whitford took a deep breath and crossed her arms. "I don't think your unfinished proofreading will hold up production, Ted. However, Felix and Miriam will be desperate to get Yulleg back. His autograph is the cornerstone of their fortunes. They are going to want him for public appearances. But, more importantly, I need that book. I want to ensure our secrets are carefully cloaked."

Ted scuffed his shoe along the stone floor. "I don't make public appearances, and it doesn't cause my publishers any problems."

"You're not famous," said Ms. Whitford. "Not like Yulleg. You are not in his league. People love prodigies. He's outselling everyone, even you with all your combined pen names and titles."

Ted stopped scuffing his shoe and looked up at Ms. Whitford. "I've sold plenty of books this year!"

"Really? When is the last time you cashed a royalty cheque?"

Ted blinked, thinking. "I don't know. I've been too busy keeping an eye on Yulleg to notice, which is more than I can say for you!"

As the adults continued arguing, Yulleg came over to Polly. "I'm Yulleg Snoblivski."

Polly groaned. "Duh. I know who you are."

"I made you this," he said, opening his palm and showing her the dragon pendant. "I sent one of my assistants to deliver this to you at your apartment but—"

This time Polly shoved Yulleg in the chest. He dropped the pendant and stumbled, trying to keep his feet beneath him. "Don't you ever speak to me. Not ever! Not even when we're back at school! I don't care how famous you are!"

Everyone stopped talking and stared at Polly and Yulleg.

"Ah...to be young and in love," said Polly's dad, breaking the tension. All the adults within earshot chuckled, except Ms. Whitford.

Ted bent down and picked up the necklace. "You remind me of a friend and I, back when we were young and foolish and about your age."

"Dad! He almost stabbed me, and he almost killed me with that letter bomb!"

"Only because he's got a crush on you, and who could blame him? You're very cute. Here," he said handing Polly the pendant. "Just wear it. It's impressive. And if you ask me, it looks like Xelif. It's a nice gift for a young girl, and he made it himself. That counts for something. Put it on, and let's see how pretty you look."

Polly shook her head and shoved it away. "You wear it then if you think it's so nice."

"Don't mind if I do." Ted accepted the necklace and put it on.

Yulleg's face was red. "Give that back. No one said it was yours. Polly can't just give it away like that."

"Apparently, she can, kid. And I'm wearing it for good luck."

"Right," said Ms. Whitford. "We have work to do. Ted, take your team of writers and head down to the landing bay."

"Do I get to go?" said Polly.

"No!" said Ms. Whitford and her dad together.

Ms. Whitford put on a headset and nodded to indicate she was ready to have it switched on. She looked flustered. "You have a lot more writing to do, Polly, before you can join the Guild and become part of all this nonsense."

"What about Yulleg? Why does he get to go? He's not even in the Guild," Polly protested.

"Yulleg is going to Mightright because he might be able to bargain with Felix and Miriam to stop production and let me review the book. We don't want to get in a fight over it. We just want a copy of the production file to look over. That's all."

Ms. Whitford gave the writer at the controls a thumbs up. "I've got to focus now so I can guide your father and his team through Mightright's labyrinth. I do hope these diagrams are still current." She turned away from Polly and leaned over a set of large papers with drawings of the interior layout of the building.

Polly watched as Ms. Whitford ran her finger along the blue lines. She shifted her weight, and her shoes made a grinding sound on the stone floor.

Ms. Whitford snapped her head up. "You're still here? You have some focusing to do yourself, young lady. Use those visualization exercises and get writing! I'm starting to think you will never get your first draft written. I need you to prove me wrong. Show me you are a writer."

Polly nodded and began to walk away, but then she stopped and cleared her throat.

"Make it quick," said Ms. Whitford, not looking up from the diagrams.

"What about those girls at Dr. Mammozarack's clinic? May I take Scrum and go get them?"

"Leave that to the Guild, Polly. I don't want to see you until you have finished all the work I left on your desk."

"Yes. Ms. Whitford. I will."

CHAPTER THIRTEEN

An Important Mission

Polly and Scrum crept up a sloped, torch-lit hallway toward the landing bay. Scrum's stomach gurgled loudly.

"Sh!" hissed Polly, yanking his beard.

"Ouch! That hurts!"

"Sh, I said! I don't know if the landing bay is empty or not. There are probably guards—oh, Scrum, the smell." Polly plugged her nose and started breathing through her mouth. "What did you eat?"

"The usual, plus I tried a new dessert. It was scrumptious, even tastier than laptops."

"Was it rotten eggs or something?"

Scrum stuck out his tongue cheekily at Polly. "No! After dinner, one of the writers came into the dining hall and made sure every dragon ate a bowl of pens with ink sauce."

"They are going to smell us before they see us. Do you feel okay?" Polly stopped to examine him.

"I feel okay." As Scrum spoke, his voice wavered. "It's just a little indigestion. I'll walk it off."

"Did all the dragons eat it?"

"Yes, they had to."

"Had to? That doesn't sound right." Polly looked at Scrum. "Did any of the others get sick?"

Scrum shook his head and shrugged.

Polly wondered if something was wrong but then put it out of her mind. It was Guild business, as Ms. Whitford would undoubtedly say. "Can you fly?"

Scrum nodded weakly, and they continued their quiet progress up the hallway.

The landing bay was empty when Scrum and Polly arrived, which was lucky because Scrum's gas was getting worse and was starting to make Polly's vision blurry and her body feel heavy and sleepy. She yawned, which triggered a yawn from Scrum.

"My tail is really heavy. How come I never noticed that before?"

Polly yawned again. "I dunno."

Polly stood in the centre of the landing bay and looked at the signs above all the portals. The letters were swimming in the air and appeared to be written in a language she did not recognize. She tried to focus so she could see which portal led to the depression clinic for teen girls. She rubbed her eyes with leaden arms one last time and collapsed to the stone floor next to Scrum, who was already snoring peacefully.

★

The Mongolian night air was bracing and shrouded with stars. Ted and Xelif flew point, leading a team of writers to Mightright's corporate headquarters in the Altai Mountains. He was getting annoyed because the dragons were sluggish, and their air speed was unusually slow. He was just about to bark the order to double their speed, when he heard one of the writers calling him from behind.

"Sir! My dragon...there's something wrong with him. It's like he's flying through syrup. His wings are slowing. I think he's falling asleep. We're going to fall."

Yulleg, who was sitting behind Ted on Xelif's back trying to protect himself from the freezing wind, looked down at the rugged mountain peaks. He dug his fingers into Ted's stomach.

Laura Michelle Thomas

Ted grimaced, ignored the sudden pain, and leaned forward to speak into Xelif's ears. "Get us down somewhere solid, quickly!"

"Ted!" said Ms. Whitford in his earpiece. "What's going on out there?"

"Not sure. The dragons are slow, sleepy, not Xelif though. He appears to be fine at the moment. We're going to land as soon as we find a safe place."

Xelif banked right and aimed for a high peak with a flat ledge on one side. He began a regular circular descent, when he noticed one of the younger dragons was already sound asleep and quickly losing altitude. Xelif left his position at the point, circled back, flew underneath the small dragon, and took her up on his back. With the dragon on board, Yulleg's body was mashed into Ted's back, pushing Ted halfway up Xelif's thin neck, where it was much harder to hold on.

"Land, Xelif! Hurry!"

"Ted?" said Ms. Whitford.

"Stand by," said Ted as Xelif dove straight for the peak. The other dragons followed him. "Hang on tight!"

Yulleg gripped Ted's waist as hard as he could, anxious to be on solid ground.

Xelif cut his descent short and hit the mountain top with too much speed. Ted and Yulleg managed to hang on, but the sleeping dragon and her writer were catapulted to the ground. The rest of the team touched down on the flat side of the snow-dotted peak, and everyone dismounted. Within moments, every dragon, except Xelif, was snoring loudly.

"What's that awful smell?" asked Yulleg.

Ted inhaled deeply. The smell was foul, indeed. It also made him feel strange and heavy. "It's poison— some kind of sleeping gas! Cover your mouths and noses. Move as far away as you can from the dragons." Ted spotted a flat piece of ground with a rocky over-hang partially covering it. "Follow me. Xelif, you too. Masterteller, are you hearing this?"

Ms. Whitford spoke into the team's headsets. "Yes. And I think you should know that Polly was just brought up to the great hall. She and Scrum were found unconscious in the landing bay. One of the writers who tried to lift Scrum on to a stretcher passed out from the dragon's gas. You've got to get the team away from those dragons."

"We are," said Ted. "Hurry!"

The team of three women and three men, plus Yulleg, followed Ted and Xelif down to the covered patch of ground. Out of smelling range, everyone seemed suddenly more alert, but concern for their dragons was written on every face.

Ted addressed the team. "Here's what we're going to do. The kid and I are going to carry on. The rest of you build a fire and keep warm until the dragons wake up. If they wake up soon, follow us to Mightright. If they don't, and you are still here when we have the book, we'll come back and help you figure out how to get back to the portal."

"Ted, you are not authorized to do this alone," said Ms. Whitford, her voice cutting though his earpiece. "You are to stay together as a group, and we'll come get you."

"Roger that," said Ted. He promptly took off his headset and handed it to one of the women. "Let's go, Yulleg."

As Xelif rose up over the peak, they could hear the others calling after them, begging them to come back.

"This is crazy," said Yulleg.

"Not really, kid. They're writers not fighters, masters with words in fictional worlds, but when it comes to real life conflict... Have you ever been in a fight, kid?"

"Not really," Yulleg admitted, "unless you count the punch your daughter gave me back at the Guild."

Ted laughed loudly. "That's my girl. I'm starting to regret I missed so much of her life."

"I'm sure you can make up for it, once she forgives you for lying to her about being a tractor salesman."

Ted whistled. "That was stupid of me."

Yulleg chuckled. "I'll say. Where did you get the idea anyway?"

"I grew up on a wheat farm. My siblings are doctors, engineers, and professors. They all made fun of my mother's attempts at poetry when we were growing up, not a lot of respect for the arts. Let's just leave it at that."

Yulleg looked down at the desolate, snow-crusted ground. "How are we going to find the production room and stop the print run? What's your plan?"

"I haven't figured that out yet," Ted confessed. "Luck, maybe?"

A tall building that squatted like a giant on the side of a mountain was rapidly coming into view. It looked like every light in the place was on. Yulleg whistled. "That place has more windows than any building I've ever seen. And it looks like they're waiting for us."

Ted didn't answer.

As they flew closer to Mightright, which had been built right into the mountainside, Yulleg realized he was wrong about the lights. What he thought were lights coming though uncovered windows were actually thousands of wooden torches that had been outfitted with electric lights. The building seemed to have been constructed out of an equal mix of ancient and ultra-modern materials except for glass. It was made of stone and steel and was part castle, part skyscraper.

Xelif banked, flew over the roof, and landed on a small outcropping of rock just above the building. Ted slid off Xelif's back and lay down on the ground so he could peer over the ledge. It had started snowing. Yulleg shivered as he stood beside Ted's prone form.

"I think if we use that root we can climb down and get on to the roof unnoticed. There's no one down there, so if we go now, we might just make it inside without setting off any alarms."

"What if the whole place is alarmed, including the roof?"

"Yulleg, you just gave me a great idea." Ted pushed himself back up to his feet. "Forget about sneaking in. We're going to set off the alarm and let them know we're here. That'll be the fastest way in and the fastest way to the production room. Felix will probably take us there, tie us up to the printing press, and give a ripping villain speech, or maybe Miriam will. Who knows? Let's go find out. Xelif!"

The great dragon lowered himself so they could climb on. Yulleg didn't move. This could jeopardize his freedom. He had no intention of being caught and cajoled into writing more books.

"Suit yourself, kid, but it's mighty cold out here, and sunrise is still a long way off."

Ted was right. It was cold, too cold to stay out on a Mongolian mountain top all night. Yulleg looked at the stubby, snow-frosted evergreens. Who knew how long it would take for anyone to find him? "I'll go, but you have to promise to get me out again. I'm done with writing. This is the last thing I'm going to do for you, for the Guild, for anyone. You have to swear on Polly's life you will get me out."

"I hear you, kid. Don't worry. We'll come out of this just fine."

Yulleg swung his leg over Xelif's back and wrapped his arms around Ted's waist.

"Xelif. I want you to land with a bang. Let them know they've got company."

Xelif nodded and launched straight up into the frozen sky.

"What if he doesn't stop in time?" cried Yulleg when he realized what the dragon was planning to do.

Xelif reached the pinnacle of his climb and then gently turned his nose downward to start the dive. In the brief moment of weightlessness that came before the harrowing descent, Ted spoke calmly. "Dive, my old friend, and make it a good one."

Xelif nodded and dove straight at the roof. Yulleg screamed and closed his eyes, fighting to hang on against the rushing wind.

"Wings! Xelif! Brake! Brake!" Ted was no longer so nonchalant about slamming into the stone roof.

A split second before his face smashed into the roof, Xelif arched his back and spread his wings like air brakes. Arching his body nearly into a complete circle made his hefty rear end slam into the glistening metal pipes that crisscrossed the roof. Unable to come to a complete stop, the dragon continued upwards and did a graceful backwards loop before slamming once again, this time on all fours, onto the roof. Yulleg heard the stones and pipes crack beneath them.

"That ought to do it," said Ted, hopping off.

"Yeah," said Yulleg, trying to catch his breath. "I'm pretty sure they know we're here. Don't forget your promise."

★

The production room at Mightright was humming, as the gigantic offset printing presses were readied to start producing the first million copies of *Dragon by a Tale* at the heady rate of 9,600 pages per minute. Felix balanced on a stool beside a series of control panels that faced the massive refrigerator-shaped machines. He looked to his left and admired the long row of blue and dull-grey steel. Black dials and switches dotted the sides of every giant box. He looked back at the press manager, who was flicking switches and tapping keys. "Hey!" Felix shouted in the man's ear. "How long until we can get started?"

The man at the panel—a grizzled self-published writer, who had recently taken a job at Mightright to support his wife and put his two kids through trade school—pushed his black skull cap higher on his forehead and pointed at an antique hourglass-shaped timer suspended from the centre of the ceiling. A digital display in the top bulb showed how much time was left until the press was ready to start printing. The current time to go was five minutes.

"Can't we speed this up?" bellowed Felix.

The man shook his head and continued turning dials and typing data into the machine.

Felix was edgy, so edgy he had ordered the press manager to skip printing a sample copy before programming the entire print run. Once started, the press could not be stopped until the entire run of one million books was complete—except in the case of a power failure.

Earlier, the senior executives at Mightright had argued vociferously with Dr. Mammozarack saying it was foolhardy, insane even, to run one million copies of something that had not been subject to final testing and approval. It was easy for something to go awry on the first run: a plate could slip and start printing pages with words running over the edge of the pages, pages could be run into the binding machine upside down or backwards, and the list went on. The doctor had listened to their protests for all of two minutes before she ordered everyone, except the press manager, to be locked up in the warehouse beneath the building.

The digital display in the top bulb of the hour glass blinked. Four minutes to go.

Felix peered over the shoulder of the press manager to assure himself everything was looking good. Most of what was displayed on the screen was gobbledygook to him, but there was an icon in the top right hand corner of the screen that was flashing a message: *Preparing to Print*. The man had told him that the message had to change to *Now Printing* before the first page of the first copy of the novel would run.

There was also a small image showing the front cover of the book on the computer screen. Felix smiled, and a tiny tear bubbled up to the corner of one of his eyes. He had never stopped loving the beautiful dragon depicted on the cover. He had the publisher hire the finest illustrator in the world to bring his Quill to life. At last, her

Laura Michelle Thomas

tragic tale would be told. He smiled, remembering the last time he saw her, that tender moment in the laboratory when he had reached his snout through the bars of her cage and kissed her goodbye.

Three minutes.

Felix focused every ounce of his attention, energy, and breath on the flashing message: *Preparing to Print.* He glanced up at the clock and willed time to move faster and the machine to spontaneously start the print run early.

"Felix! Felix!" shouted Dr. Mammozarack, coming up behind him. When the dragon did not respond, she thumped him on the stump of his tail.

Felix yelped, lost his balance, and fell backwards, landing on the press room floor like an upside down turtle. He scrambled and scratched and twisted and turned until he was at last standing.

"We have visitors," said the doctor.

Two minutes.

"Who?" growled Felix.

"Ted and the boy are back."

"I thought you sent the Guild another surprise that would stop them from interfering with production?"

"I did! But apparently your big brother has an iron stomach."

Felix snorted. "What did you do with them?"

"Look up there."

The boardroom had floor-to-ceiling widows running the length of the production floor. Ted, Yulleg, and Xelif looked down on Felix and the doctor.

One minute.

"I love these moments. Put me on the counter. I must be able to see the screen."

"Certainly." The doctor bent down and picked Felix up. She placed him gently on the counter next to the press manager. "I'm glad the secrecy is finally over," she said. "I am actually looking forward to reading this new book of yours, Felix. Let's just hope it keeps us all flush." Dr. Mammozarack leaned forward, with an uncharacteristic smile lighting up her face, and looked closely at the screen. "I'm going to need money to fund—is that Quill on the cover?"

Felix smiled. He had won. She was too late to stop the truth from coming out.

Zero.

The words *Now Printing* blinked at him.

"How dare you!" shouted Dr. Mammozarack over the rising hum.

Felix spun around and faced her. "She was the greatest dragon I have ever known, and you caged her and abused her right up until the day she died. She never got to go outside because of you. The world needs to know her story, and there is nothing you can do to stop it now."

The great machines revved up and whirred even louder as they started taking up paper. Felix was smiling, his small body awash with relief. One million copies in a single run. One million pictures of Quill. It made his heart ache with joy.

The lights dimmed, flickered, and went out. The press sputtered and ground to a halt. The room became deafeningly quiet, except for Felix who yelled, "No!"

Upstairs in the boardroom, it was pitch black.

"Stay calm, kid, and give the dragon some room." Ted called to Xelif. "I need you to warm up your fire and get a good glow on. Gently though, just a glow, not a spark. We only need a little light so we can find a way out of here."

The sucking sound of Xelif's deep inhalation filled the boardroom. The dragon's midsection began to glow with an orange heat, causing the temperature in the room to go up by several degrees.

"Easy, Xelif. Easy." Ted turned to Yulleg who was on the other side of the angular steel table. "He won't be able to hold the glow for long, kid. The pressure he's feeling right now to belch fire is virtually unstoppable. Search for anything that looks like a way out. Quickly!"

As Yulleg searched the room, Ted tried the steel doors again, thinking the power outage might have released them. But they wouldn't budge. Evidently, the board-room was a safe room meant to be kept securely locked in the event of an emergency. He had no idea where the controls might be.

Sweat dripped into Ted's eyes as he felt for hinges or anything small that could be loosed, opened, or turned. He glanced at Xelif. The dragon was going cross-eyed from concentrating so hard. His belly glowed a deeper shade of orange and pulsed like a small sun.

"Stop, Xelif," Ted commanded. The last thing they needed was to start a fire.

The dragon exhaled as slowly as he could, then collapsed on the floor exhausted. His glow faded, and it should have been pitch black in the boardroom again, but it wasn't. A flickering orange glow came from the production floor. Ted and Yulleg ran to the glass windows and looked down. The overhead sprinkler system was on in the production room, and droplets of water were starting to patter against the widows.

The press manager was using a fire extinguisher to put out a fire in the control panel, but it wasn't helping. The flames were taller than the man. Felix was hopping up and down on the counter, shouting. Dr. Mammozarack was nowhere to be seen.

Yulleg sighed with relief. "That's it then, mission accomplished. Let's get out of here."

"Ha. Nothing's ever that easy. They'll have other copies, other press machines. All it will do is buy the Masterteller the time she needs to review the manuscript, assuming we can get our hands on a copy."

Yulleg suddenly remembered something. He stuck his hands in his pockets, searching the front and back of his jeans. "I'm such an idiot!"

"What are you talking about?"

"The flash drive. I had it in my pocket the day we escaped from my house. It's got the final draft of *Dragon by a Tale* on it. But I don't have it. It must have fallen out of my pocket somewhere."

"Are you absolutely sure?"

Yulleg nodded. "I put the story on the flash drive and deleted the master copy on my laptop. I was going to use it to bargain with Felix for my freedom. But then he busted into my room with the envelope, and I lost my nerve and stuck it in my pocket. Now it's gone. I don't have it."

"Probably wouldn't have made a difference anyway, kid." Ted put his hand on Yulleg's shoulder. "They've got copies of copies and backups of backups. I'm sure."

"You're probably right. Felix obviously had a copy to do this run with. It was a brain-dead idea. I don't know why I thought it would work."

"Don't be so hard on yourself, kid. It was done in the name of freedom. I get it. The desire for freedom, it makes us do strange things."

So now what?" Yulleg pushed on a leather chair and watched it roll away from him. We're still trapped."

"I think, if we ask nicely, we can get Xelif to pick up one of these fancy chairs with his tail and get him to throw it through one of these big windows." Ted tapped the glass and peered out through the water droplets. "Never mind the fancy chair, I think his head is hard enough. And this room is long enough for a flying start. We just have to make sure we don't crash into that hourglass up there."

Yulleg's mouth was wide open. "You can't be serious."

"Climb on, kid. Let's go get wet."

CHAPTER FOURTEEN

Wannabe

Polly sat at her work table in the great hall with a wool blanket pulled up over her head like a tent. She shivered, still feeling the effects of the ice-bath Ms. Whitford had used to rouse her. She twirled her pencil on its point to see how long she could keep it upright. Her trembling hands made it difficult to get a good spin. In front of her were two sheets of paper. One paper had handwritten instructions from Ms. Whitford:

First, write three short paragraphs: one that summarizes your plot, one that describes your main character, and one that describes your main setting. Second, write out each of the scenes you visualized in the dark hall (introduction, climax and ending). Give yourself five minutes to write each one. Use the timer I left on your desk. Third, complete the "focusing" worksheet. Don't over think it. This is just an exercise that will help you write your first draft—your lump of clay. And, Polly, do not let Scrum interfere with your work. I know you two have been getting along, but this is not his time. It's yours. Trust me, if you give him a chance to critique your work, he will. It is his nature to challenge your ideas. Once you have completed these tasks you may begin writing your first draft. Write hot and fast and have fun. You shouldn't have any problem finishing.

The focusing worksheet had a list down the left side of the paper and was blank on the right side where Polly was to fill in information about her story.

> Working Title:
> Genre:
> Category:
> Theme:
> Audience
> Tone:
> Purpose:
> Point of View:
> Main Setting:
> Atmosphere:
> Hook:
> Protagonist:
> Protagonist's Need:
> Protagonist's Allies:
> Protagonist's Enemies:
> Conflict:
> Climax:
> Ending:
> Protagonist's Growth:

Polly thought this was starting to feel too much like a school exercise, so she got up and called for Scrum. She had some unfinished business to take care of, business far more important than writing.

While Polly had been thinking about writing, Scrum was thinking about his stomach. He rummaged around the empty great hall looking for scraps. He was starving, and the dragon dining hall had been shut down until all the food could be tested for traces of the sleeping ink. He ran his nose along the stone floor, sniffing. He hoped to find a juicy piece of wire under the tables and desks.

As he sniffed around the empty chairs tucked along the edges of the stone meeting table, he caught a scent and followed it across the room over to the wall underneath the massive screens. There he found a

Laura Michelle Thomas

silver-coloured flash drive. It smelled wonderful, and he lapped at it until it was wedged against the wall, and he could get a grip on it. Once it was in his mouth, he held it on his tongue, savouring the metallic flavour.

"What have you got in your mouth, young dragon?"

Scrum snapped his jaws shut and swallowed.

He turned around to face the woman who had been charged with monitoring the screens while Ms. Whitford and the others were away.

"What's going on?" asked Polly.

"Nothing. See." Scrum opened his jaws and stuck out his long tongue.

"Gross," said Polly, grimacing. She looked sheepishly at the writer. "I'm sorry about that. He won't disturb you again." She turned to Scrum. "Follow me. There is something we need to do."

Scrum held his head high as he walked past the writer.

"What are you up to, Polly?" the woman asked as she sat down in a chair and flicked a switch. A map of Mongolia came into view. "You were given strict instructions to write your first draft, I believe."

"I know. We're going. C'mon, Scrum."

As they walked back across the great hall to Polly's alcove, Scrum broke the silence. "You want me to help you work on your vamperwolf story? I thought I was supposed to just watch you write."

"We're going to the landing bay."

"No, we're not."

Polly looked over her shoulder to see if the woman was watching. She wasn't. She had her headset on, and her back was to Polly's work table. She was busy pulling up evermore detailed maps of Mongolia.

Polly whispered, "We're going to finish what we started and rescue those girls at the clinic."

"That's a bad idea. There's no one here to help us if we get in trouble again. And if we get caught, they won't even know where we are. Besides, you're supposed to be writing."

"Quiet, Scrum. We're going. Yulleg Snoblivski isn't the only one around here who gets to go on a mission."

★

Polly poked her head just high enough out of the water-like surface of the reflecting pool to see if the courtyard was clear. It was. She reached down and tapped Scrum on his knobby forehead. The dragon surfaced noisily beside her and sputtered, "This is a bad idea. You should be working on your story."

"Sh," said Polly, easing herself up onto the ancient brickwork.

Scrum hoisted his long body up beside her. "Even if we can get them out of here, there's no way I can carry all those girls through the portal."

"Really, Scrum? Stop being such a Negative Nelly. Your back is longer than any dragon I have ever seen. You could carry my entire English class on your back and still have room to spare."

Scrum sniggered.

"What's so funny?" Scrum's comments had really started to grate on her nerves.

"You wanting to be a writer." Scrum looked up at the overcast night sky.

Polly followed his gaze upward. "Why is that so funny?"

"Because since I met you, you've hardly done any writing. You say you want to be a writer, but here we are rescuing other wannabe writers so you can get out of writing." Scrum turned his back on Polly and started walking across the unlit courtyard toward the entrance.

"That's not true!"

Scrum looked back at Polly. He sniggered again. "Oh yes, it is. It's what we literary dragons call situational irony. If this was a scene in a novel and someone was reading this right now and saw how blind you are to your fear, or whatever it is that is stopping you from writing, they would be laughing out loud. Look at you—you're a wannabe rescuing wannabes."

Polly glared at Scrum. She'd always had trouble understanding the difference between the three types of irony—situational, verbal, and dramatic. To cover her ignorance, she smiled, pretending she got the joke. "Very funny." Polly rudely pushed past Scrum to be the first to the door. "Let's just go do what we came here to do, minus the commentary."

Scrum chuckled to himself. "Imagine a girl, who wants to be writer, giving up her own writing time so she can liberate other girls who want to be writers too. In the end, she does not become a writer at all, but the other girls do. It's the opposite of what our protagonist expects and desires. And all the while she doesn't see it, but the reader does. Now that's what I call situational irony, with a touch of dramatic irony thrown in for good measure."

Polly grabbed hold of Scrum's beard and yanked him through the open door. "Stop muttering to yourself, and get in here!"

★

Ms. Whitford and her team of a dozen writers—including the ones Ted had abandoned on the mountain peak, which they had picked up en route—were in the warehouse arguing with the executives of Mightright Publishing Company. It had been easy to get in. When the power had gone out, all the exterior doors automatically unlocked. Water poured from the sprinklers, and hundreds of thousands of books awaiting shipment were rapidly getting ruined.

"Look at the inventory you've destroyed with that little trick!" said Mightright's CEO. He zeroed in on Ms. Whitford, held his face right up to hers, and jammed an index finger in her direction. "First, that insane doctor locks us up down here so she can start a million-copy book run without printing a test copy. Do you know we haven't even seen the book? Not a page! Not a synopsis or chapter outline! This deal was entirely put together on our good faith and—"

"You mean your greed," said Ms. Whitford, calmly. She took her glasses off, reached into an interior pocket of her suede cloak, and pulled out a handkerchief to dry them off. "Yulleg's a cash cow, nothing more, but nothing less. I suspect you would print just about anything you could reasonably put his name to."

The CEO's sharp features flushed. He yanked out his own handkerchief and swiped the water off his forehead. "Then you boobs from the Guild come along and shut off the power. And somewhere in this building," he sputtered, "you've started a fire. For all I know this place is going up in an inferno!"

"But, this isn't our fault, it's—"

"But nothing! This will be the end of your organization. You and your writers will never get another deal with any publisher on the planet. Not when I'm through dealing with this fiasco."

The Mightright executives murmured and nodded in agreement.

Ms. Whitford stepped steadily forward forcing the CEO to step backwards until his back was up against a tower of brown cardboard boxes filled with soggy books. "The truth is we don't need companies like Mightright. Stories don't need to be printed. Stories can be told so well they burn into a listener's memory forever. We are not afraid to go back to those days."

This was a lie. Ms. Whitford knew printed books were a critical part of modern culture. Not being able to sell their stories in print format would devastate the Guild. No one could make a decent living working strictly with oral tellings of their work, not in today's world.

"Get ready to take a trip back in time," sneered the CEO. "We are going to stop printing the Guild's books. I swear. We'll only work with rogues like Yulleg, and that crazy doctor, Mammozarack, if she can ever get a book done."

Ms. Whitford cringed.

The CEO continued. "*Dragon by a Tale* will be published and distributed worldwide by the end of the week. We have the production file, and the doctor has the boy."

"We have Yulleg, actually." Ms. Whitford observed the man's face. Thick blue veins rose up to criss-cross his pinched temples. She jabbed deeper with her words. "He says he's written enough. He wants out. This is Yulleg Snoblivski's last book, if it meets our approval."

"You wouldn't." The hand holding the soggy handkerchief hung limp at the CEO's side. "Our shareholders, they'll kill me."

Ms. Whitford backed up slightly and crossed her arms. "I wouldn't be surprised if they did kill you. But, from the Guild's point of view, they should be thanking you for all the money you've made off the boy. His short career has made you all rich. Gratitude would be more appropriate."

With tight lips, a white face, and veins bulging, the CEO stepped around Ms. Whitford. She let him pass and nodded to her team to do the same. He led his staff and the other executives out through the open door. They followed obediently, single file, their feet splashing through the growing puddles on the warehouse floor.

★

Polly and Scrum stood in the dining hall staring at the perfectly clean, perfectly empty glass table. Everything had been repaired or replaced since Scrum had broken through two walls during their escape, and the place was eerily quiet. Scrum opened and closed his wings. The web-like chandelier swung slightly and tinkled softly.

Polly looked around and shrugged at the emptiness. "They must be in bed."

"I still say this is foolish. You should be at the Guild doing the work Ms. Whitford left for you."

Polly dismissed his suggestion with a wave. "Tomorrow. Promise. Follow me."

Polly led them out into a white corridor. They walked for a long time. Polly searched for a door, an elevator, a stairwell, but found nothing, nothing but more white hallways. It was like a maze, and no matter which way she turned, they ended up back where they started. They didn't even come across any of the pink-clad nurses.

After the seventh time they arrived back in the empty dining hall, Polly walked over to the table and sat down in the same chair she had sat in before. She looked up, expecting the black cylinder to start lowering down, but it didn't. The room was forsaken, tomb-like, except for the tinkling of the creepy chandelier, which continued despite the unnatural stillness of the air.

Polly looked at Scrum. "I don't get it. They were here."

Scrum, who had been standing near the entrance, came over to her. His face was stern, and his ears twitched nervously. "You're not supposed to be here. That's why the setting is so empty. I can feel it in my backbone, from my skull all the way to the spade of my tail. We have to leave."

"What do you know, stupid dragon?" Polly put her head down on the table.

"Enough to see you are on the brink of realizing the truth."

Polly's voice came back muffled. "What truth?"

"That despite the fact you have me—a gifted literary dragon—inside you, you don't have what it takes to be a writer. Eventually, you will go insane trying to put up with me. Then you'll take your own life and kill us both, or we will end up in a place like this."

Polly lifted her head. "You're wrong."

"But here we are, in this awful place, chasing after wannabe writers who don't exist."

"But, they were here. You saw them."

"But they aren't here now." Scrum turned to leave. "Let's go."

Polly stood up. "Fine." She followed him out of the dining hall.

At the door, Scrum belched. "I don't feel so good."

Polly put her hands on her hips. "I knew you ate something off the floor in the great hall!"

"Just a little flash drive. I've tried them before, just the other day. But this one's not sitting right. I'm queasy."

"Someday, I'm going to get you off electronics entirely."

Scrum tried to smile. "Good—"

"What was that?" whispered Polly. Goosebumps prickled her skin.

"Someone's coming," said Scrum.

Polly hurried Scrum outside and climbed on his back. The albino dragon flew straight up in the sky, stopped, turned his nose down, and began to dive. Polly closed her eyes, leaned forward, and hugged Scrum's neck. She was getting used to the touch of his cold scales on her skin and the sensation of her stomach flying up into her throat.

CHAPTER FIFTEEN

A Bad Sign

A smoky haze reached from waist height to the high ceiling of Mightright's primary production room. The emergency power had kicked in, illuminating the room with thin blue light. Water pattered down on the steel press.

Ted and Yulleg jumped off Xelif's back and walked over to Felix. The tiny dragon looked even more hideous wet than he did dry. The water made his scarred skin look glossy, almost plastic. He stood near the control panel, gripping the press manager's leg with his claws, wailing at him to get the press up and running.

"Felix!" said Ted. "We've got to get out of here!"

The press manager looked over at Ted and nodded.

Felix, however, ignored him and shook the man's leg violently, asking if there was another functional press in the building.

"Yes. In the sub-basement. It's old. But it'll be dry down there. They never installed sprinklers. It can be ready to go as soon as full power is restored. That shouldn't take long. I just need another copy of the production file."

Felix dropped his grip on the man's leg. "You have aother copy, don't you?"

"Ah...let's see...no...I was never given one. You gave me the production copy on a flash drive, but look at it now." He pointed to a black blob sticking out of the computer. "That was the only copy I had. Surely," he smiled nervously, "you must have another one."

"Didn't you run a back up before we started?" asked Felix.

"Of course! But it was on this same computer. We can see if it can be salvaged from the hard drive. But it's still smouldering."

All eyes turned to the control panel. The computer screen was black and sooty, the black knobs and switches had melted into streaks on the face of the panel. Tendrils of smoke wafted into the air from cracks in the computer's casing.

"Where is Miriam?" said Ms. Whitford, striding into the room with the rest of her team following closely. Their cloaks were darkly stained around their chests and shoulders, and their hair hung in thick chunks across their grim faces. She walked directly over to Felix and picked him up.

Felix wiggled and twisted, trying break free. "You can't do this to me! Put me down!"

"Watch it, Patti!" yelled Ted. "His stomach is glowing."

"Sorry, Felix," said Ms. Whitford. "We need you back at headquarters so we can get to the bottom of this." She handed Felix, who was thrashing wildly, to one of the writers. "Muzzle him, take him outside, and tie him to his brother's back."

The writer nodded, quickly threw a muzzle around Felix's snout, and went out with the others.

"Miriam's gone," Ted told Ms. Whitford as they followed the team out of the production room.

Ms. Whitford frowned. "I wonder if she knows what the book is about now."

Yulleg piped up. "I think so. She and Felix were arguing about something, just before the power went off."

"What about me?" called the production manager. He had followed them into the hallway. "Can I come?"

Ted looked at Ms. Whitford. "Self-published authors? Have we sunk so low?"

Ms. Whitford stopped abruptly and turned on Ted. "Remember the oath you took? Whatever it takes to get a well-written, well-edited book into reader's hands, the world needs stories—ringing any bells? Whether a writer chooses to sign with corporate giants like Mightright for a ten-percent royalty deal or hand-copy pages to sell for a few pennies on a street corner, we make no distinction. We acknowledge that some writers have sales skills and others do not. We're not in it for the money. And if you had stuck around these past ten years instead of going off on your own literary joy ride, you might understand." She paused and waited for Ted to apologize. When he didn't, she glared at him and continued. "Of course, the man is welcome! He is a writer. He has a dragon. That's all that matters."

"I do. I have a dragon," said the press manager, stepping forward. He took off his skull cap and twisted it in his hands. "But I'm afraid he needs some work. I confess...it's been a struggle." Tears moistened the red rims of the man's eyes.

Ms. Whitford reached into her cloak, took out a notepad and pen, and wrote some instructions on it. She tore out the page and handed it to the man. "You cannot come with us right now, but here's how to find us."

He bowed and nodded. "Thank you. Thank you very much."

Ted kept his mouth shut and followed Ms. Whitford and Yulleg outside. He didn't dare engage her in conversation until she cooled off.

Though the fire was out in the production room, smoke still wafted out the open doors on the main floor. The sun was coming up over the toothy Mongolian peaks and lighting up the snow-crusted desert. Felix was in the middle of the grounds that formed the building's main entryway. He was strapped to Xelif's back.

Xelif, in turn, was tethered to each of the other dragons, except for a gargantuan alabaster dragon standing apart from the others. Encircled as he was by a kaleidoscope of dragons in all shapes and sizes, Felix looked like a wilted blossom at the top of a maypole.

"What's with the tethers on Xelif?" asked Ted, gruffly.

"Just a precaution. I mean no disrespect to the bond you have with your dragon, but there is something about Felix that worries me. We still don't know why he is alive. I want to be sure we get him back to headquarters."

Ted said nothing and walked over to Xelif, who stood with his head hung so low his nose almost touched the frozen ground.

"Sorry, old friend. It's just until we get back to headquarters. We need to find out what's wrong with your brother." Ted scratched Xelif's side, climbed up behind Felix, and grasped the struggling dragon between his thighs.

"That dragon is whiter than snow," said Yulleg, pointing at Ms. Whitford's dragon.

Despite the situation, or perhaps because of it, everyone burst out laughing.

"Wow. I thought you were a prodigy." Ted laughed.

"What do you mean?" Yulleg's cheeks flushed.

"Whiter than snow? That cliché is so over-baked it makes my teeth ache."

Ms. Whitford smiled and climbed on the back of her massive, snake-like alabaster dragon. "You can ride with me, Yulleg. Gratidia says it's okay."

"Have you told Polly your dragon is the matriarch of Scrum's line?" Ted asked.

Ms. Whitford peered at the brighting horizon. "She needs to sell her first book before I start sharing all the Guild's secrets with her."

Ted nodded and smiled. "Do you really think she has it in her?"

"Time will tell. What about you, Ted. Do you?" Before Ted could ask her what she was referring to, Ms.

Whitford spoke to Yulleg, who was standing like a statue in the snow. "She doesn't bite, unless you're a young dragon who's not behaving. Climb on, quickly now!"

As Yulleg got up behind Ms. Whitford, the white dragon lifted her wrinkled, white face to the sun and opened her mouth. Sound poured out, filling the air with an ancient dragon chant paying homage to the coming day. All the dragons—including Felix—opened their throats and joined in the morning song.

When the air was still and quiet once more, the matriarch of Scrum's line stretched open wings three times wider than those of any other living dragon and, with a single pump, lifted herself off the ground.

As they flew across the frozen morning, Ms. Whitford had a niggling feeling something was amiss. Gratidia alone would barely fit through the portal. Binding the others together might have been a grave mistake. Ms. Whitford hoped they would be able to maneuver the strange party through the portal without incident. If they did, she would take it as a good sign, a sign life would soon return to normal.

★

Guild headquarters was deserted when Scrum touched down in the landing bay. Polly slid off his back. "This can't be a good sign. Something must have gone wrong. Maybe they're never coming back, and it's just you and me."

Scrum wasn't listening to Polly. He was too busy vomiting a clear, slippery liquid all over the floor. It formed a greasy pool under his claws.

"It's the thing you ate. I know it!" Polly was annoyed, but she also felt sorry for him. He had been extremely dizzy in the portal. More than once, he almost crashed into the rough sides. Now, he was gagging uncontrollably, but the silver flash drive seemed to have cemented itself into a corner of his elongated gut.

"Get it out of me!" gasped Scrum, his entire body heaving.

When she was sick, her mom made her drink as much water as she could swallow. Thinking this might help Scrum wash out the flash drive, Polly ran around the circumference of the landing bay looking for a firehose that might be hanging on a hook somewhere. Scrum continued to spew more slippery liquid on the floor forcing Polly, to stay near the walls.

At last, she found a low trough with an ancient wooden bucket hanging beside it. Polly wondered at such a primitive method of firefighting, then grabbed the bucket, plunged it into the cold water, and ran back to Scrum. She stayed out of the expanding puddle as long as she could but then was forced to cross it to reach him.

The substance was as slippery as ice, and she walked slowly so she wouldn't fall and spill the water. When she reached Scrum, she tried to get him to drink.

Scrum shook his head. "I can't. It won't let me."

"You want it out, right?"

Scrum's pink rimmed eyes filled with tears. He nodded.

"Then drink. All of it."

Scrum opened his jaws. Polly poured, while he forced himself to swallow. When the bucket was empty, Scrum got a strange look on his face. He began to convulse and sputter.

In her scramble to get a safe distance away from him, Polly slipped and fell. The bucket slid across the room and broke when it hit the stone wall.

Scrum bent over and started to heave.

Polly watched his snake-like body ripple violently from tail to tongue. Scrum heaved and convulsed, then heaved some more, until it came out. A silver object flew out of his open maw and sailed through the air in a majestic arc, before landing on the slippery floor, sliding into a portal, and disappearing.

Just then, on the other side of the landing bay, a portal lit up, and a pack of dragons and writers hit the slippery floor and started sliding directly at Polly and Scrum.

"Scrum!" shouted Polly. She jumped out of the way just in time to see Scrum's weak, white body disappear under the tangled mass of dragons and writers.

"Scrum?" she said, quietly. She tried to stand but couldn't, so she crawled over to the heap of human and dragon bodies that barely stirred.

"Polly?" asked Ms. Whitford, touching her head gingerly. Blood was coming from her forehead, where a large purple lump was forming. "What happened to the floor?"

Polly tried getting to her knees. "You landed on Scrum. He couldn't get out of the way and—is he going to be okay?"

Ms. Whitford was concerned. They had landed too quickly, and the slippery floor had only made things worse. It was entirely possible Scrum had been crushed by the weight of Gratidia, Xelif, and the other dragons. "Everyone, get up. Now!" As soon as she spoke she lost her footing and fell hard on her back. She didn't move.

Polly tried to stand up but she couldn't. She was covered with the slippery substance.

Though slowly regaining their wits, the writers and dragons were too stunned, and too badly injured, to move quickly. None of them could heed Ms. Whitford's order to get up.

Polly inched herself forward on her knees. "Scrum! Can you hear me?" She was filled with relief when her dad staggered into view. "Dad! Scrum's under there! Help him, please!" Polly waved and pointed at the heap of scales, cloaks, and leather straps. "Dad!"

When Ted finally noticed Polly, he nodded and turned around too quickly. He slipped, hit his head on the stone floor, and knocked himself out.

CHAPTER SIXTEEN

Cold-Hearted Writers

Polly paced back and forth outside the medical room where they were keeping Scrum. Every time she crossed in front of the windowless door, she paused, hoping someone might come out and tell her she could go inside. Polly had not been allowed to see Scrum since the accident in the landing bay. These were Ms. Whitford's orders. During one of these hopeful pauses, Yulleg loped around the corner on crutches. He had sprained his ankle in the crash.

Polly glared at him. She hadn't spoken to him since he tried to give her the dragon pendant.

"I hear you're leaving," he said casually, leaning on his crutches.

"As soon as Scrum can fly, I'm leaving this cold-hearted place and going home. Not that you care, but Ms. Whitford wanted me to 'take advantage of this time that Scrum is hurt' to write!" Polly shook with anger. "Like I said, this is a cold-hearted place, and I don't want to have anything to do with it."

"You must really hate your dad for lying to you."

Polly brushed past Yulleg and went back to pacing.

Yulleg continued. "I'd like to go home too...not home, exactly. I'd like to disappear for a while. I agree that writing isn't for everyone. They are a heartless bunch. I've had enough too."

Polly glanced at him, wondering if maybe being one of the world's most famous writers was harder than she thought. "What about your parents?"

Yulleg frowned. "I am so...I wish they had told me I was adopted, even though it wouldn't have changed anything. My real father is dead. But they should have told me. I don't care if I ever see them again."

Polly stopped pacing and faced Yulleg. "Parents who lie, I can relate. I grew up thinking my dad was a tractor salesman," she said, looking away. "Where are you going to go?"

"I'm not sure yet, but I'm leaving soon, really soon. That reminds me..." Yulleg stuck his hand in his pocket and pulled out the wooden dragon pendant. "I know you said you didn't want this, but I thought maybe, now that we're both leaving and probably won't see each other again, you might want it as a souvenir."

Polly crossed her arms and looked at the locked door that separated her from Scrum. "No, thanks. How did you get that from my dad anyway? I thought he was going to keep it."

Yulleg shrugged innocently. "I borrowed it back."

Polly caught his meaning, and it almost made her smile to think Yulleg had stolen it from her dad. She was still furious with him. "I don't want souvenirs," she sighed. "I'm not good enough to make it anyway. I don't have your talent. Even my dragon knows I can't finish a story."

Yulleg closed his fingers around the pendant. "I don't remember ever wanting to be a writer. It was just easy, so I did it."

Polly glared at Yulleg. She wanted to punch him in the guts again. It was only the crutches that stopped her. "That's ironic considering you are the most famous author on the planet. It's not fair. I can't even look at you any more. Go whittle a dragon!"

"Fine! I was just trying to be nice to the prettiest and smartest girl I have ever met. How stupid of me." He jammed the pendant back in his pocket and loped away. Over his shoulder he called, "By the way. I don't whittle; I sculpt!"

As Polly watched him go, her fury deflated. Loneliness took its place. She began to wish Yulleg would stay and keep her company. She was about to call after him, when he stopped and turned back.

"What?" she said, casually, trying not to show how relieved she was not to be alone. "Miss me already?"

Yulleg cleared his throat. "No. I came here to ask you a question about Scrum, and I forgot to ask it. What made him so sick?"

"He ate a flash drive he found on the floor in the great hall. It definitely didn't agree with him."

"Was it silver?"

"I think so. Was it yours?"

Yulleg nodded. "Can I have it back?"

"I don't have it," said Polly. "It slid into one of the portals, and I didn't see which one."

Yulleg furrowed his brow. "Does anyone else know where it went?"

"With all the injuries and everything else going on? No. Why?"

Yulleg smiled. "No reason. I just want to be the one to find it. It is mine after all."

Sensing Yulleg was holding something back, Polly crossed her arms and questioned him. "Do you know why it made Scrum so sick? I've never seen food have such an effect on him before. He's been raised on stuff like that."

Yulleg shrugged. "Maybe he's allergic to silver or flash drives in general, maybe—anyway, can you show me which portal you think it went into?"

"Maybe, but only after I see Scrum, and you have to wait with me."

Yulleg raised an eyebrow and smirked. "Are you sure you don't want the pendant? I made it just for you."

"Don't get any ideas, hot shot. I'm not one of your fans." Polly was serious about not wanting it, but she suddenly remembered Natasha's crush on Yulleg. Natasha would love to have Yulleg's pendant. Polly really missed her and looked forward to seeing her as soon as Scrum was better. Polly leaned her back against the wall and slowly slid down until she was seated on the floor. She wanted Yulleg to offer her the necklace again, but there was no way she was going to ask him directly.

Yulleg put his crutches down and took up a similar pose on the other side of the narrow stone hallway directly opposite her. Polly pretended not to notice when he took the pendant out of his pocket and started playing cat's cradle with the long leather thong. She couldn't help watching his hands. He had nice hands. The dragon, she noticed, was intricate and artful. Natasha would love it.

They sat quietly across from each other. Yulleg playing with the necklace and stealing glances at Polly; Polly pretending not to be interested, but secretly willing him to offer it to her. She broke the silence first. "Do you really want to give up your writing career? You're so famous. You have what every writer wants."

Yulleg stopped playing cat's cradle and looked directly at her. "I'm done."

"What about all your fans and your new book? You'll kill them if you just vanish."

Yulleg shrugged. "I don't care."

"Ms. Whitford told me the book is about Quill, Dr. Mammozarack's dragon. What's she like? Did you meet her?"

Yulleg stuffed the necklace in his pocket. "Quill is dead, Polly. She died a long time ago. Felix thinks it was his fault and that Quill died of a broken heart when he left the lab to come live with me. I think Mammozarack killed her. I think she made up the broken-heart story to punish Felix for becoming my dragon when I was little. But I can't prove it."

Polly's jaw fell open as the door opened and Ms. Whitford came out of the medical room, her face grim. She shut the door behind her.

Polly hopped to her feet, eager to go inside and see Scrum. "Finally!" she said, tears stinging her eyes. "I thought you were never going to let me in there!"

Ms. Whitford nodded at Yulleg, who was up and leaning on his crutches, then measured her words and spoke softly to Polly. "Scrum is extremely weak and might die. He does not want to see you."

"What? Why?" Polly was instantly furious. How dare Scrum order her around like that! "He can't tell me what to do," she fumed.

"Scrum knows," said Ms. Whitford.

"What does he know?"

"That you have decided to quit writing."

"Oh, that," said Polly, looking away. "I am going to bring Scrum home with me. We'll still be friends. Doesn't he know I still want him? Can you tell him? Please?"

"Scrum is a literary dragon. He was created to help you turn your lumps of clay into publishable master-pieces. Yes, he can breathe fire and fly and be a good friend, but if his writer does not write, he will be miser-able." Ms. Whitford looked at Polly.

Polly could read the disappointment in Ms. Whitford's eyes right through her thick glasses.

"He does not want to see you, Polly. Not ever again. You might as well leave now. There is nothing more I can do with you. Tell me when you are ready, and I'll arrange to get you back to your apartment...without Scrum. He will be staying here."

"But—"

"His mind is made up. There is nothing I can do. You need to say your goodbyes and go home."

Polly watched as Ms. Whitford walked away. When she turned the corner, Polly looked at the closed door separating her from Scrum. She reached out and put a hand on the door, imagining she could feel Scrum's cool, albino scales on her palm. Yulleg came over and put a hand on Polly's back. Polly shrugged it off. "I hate that dragon. I swear, I hate him."

★

Ms. Whitford addressed the Guild members formally. "We still do not have a copy of *Dragon by a Tale*, nor do we know where or when we might locate one. However, we do have Felix in custody, which will certainly help us get to the bottom of that book. This brings us to our next point of discussion." She paused and looked around the table at her colleagues, letting her eyes come to rest on Polly's father, who was leaning back in his chair, picking at his hangnails. "Now," continued Ms. Whitford, "we need to find Miriam and bring her in for questioning. I would like to find out what she knows about Johan's death."

"Now? Really? Ha!" said Ted, thumping his heels up on the table and putting his hands behind his head. "So you finally believe me after all these years."

Ms. Whitford's jaw tensed. "It's not a matter of believing you, Ted."

"Oh really?" he said, jumping to his feet. "Sixteen years ago, I told you that Miriam had something to do with Johan's death. Sixteen years ago, I turned down a special invitation to her lab. She invited Johan and I to watch a demonstration of some new dragon training device. Why did I turn it down? So you and I could go on our first date. I should have been there that night to protect my friend from that woman. I feel responsible. Maybe you should too, Patti."

A murmur rose around the table.

Ms. Whitford held up a hand. "You will address me as Masterteller."

The room fell silent.

She continued, "What you say is not relevant. In fact, your statement proves you do not know the truth about what happened that night, or if that is, in fact, the night Johan died. You were not there, none of us were."

All the writers around the table nodded.

"Not relevant?" spat Ted, veins bulging in his neck and on his forehead.

"Not relevant," stated Ms. Whitford, her forehead smooth, her voice even. "That is why we need Miriam to answer our questions."

Ted looked around the table, his eyes moist with tears. "Don't you understand? I might have been able to save him."

"It's not your fault," said Ms. Whitford. "No one is holding you responsible."

"I should have been there. I never trusted her, and when she was bragging about her new quick fix for unruly dragons, I should have told Johan to stop dating her."

"They were in love. There was nothing you could have done. And we do not know if she was involved in Johan's death, or in Felix's mysterious survival, or even that she is the boy's mother, as you suspect. Felix has been unconscious since the accident, and I don't want this to wait, not after what I saw in Miriam's clinic. Whether she knows anything about Johan's death or not, she must come in for questioning."

Ted continued, his voice shaking. "Johan went missing that night, and the very next day his body was found in the landing bay. If that's not suspicious, I don't know what is."

"Ted, will you go and pick up Miriam?"

"Gladly—"

"Unharmed." Ms. Whitford's voice was firm.

Ted looked defiantly at Ms. Whitford and at the other writers seated around the table. "If I do bring her here unharmed, can I trust you to actually do something this time? I told you two years ago that the rumours about Felix being Yulleg's dragon were true. I also told you who I suspected the boy's parents were, but the Guild turned a blind eye—always writers, never fighters. What assurance do I have that you will do a full investigation into Johan's death this time? Will the Guild promise to accept the truth: one of our own murdered him?"

A funnel of angry protest whirled up from the table.

Ms. Whitford's face was red with anger. "In matters of reality, the Guild will accept truth and not fiction. The only way we can establish the difference is by bringing Miriam in and letting her speak for herself."

"What if she lies again, or refuses to cooperate?" asked Ted.

The other writers looked at Ms. Whitford.

"Ted, we have our ways. We may move too slowly for your liking, but we are not imbeciles. Her lab at the clinic will be thoroughly investigated." Then Ms. Whitford addressed the room. "With your assent, ladies and gentlemen, we are adjourned so that Ted may leave immediately to bring Miriam in. All in favour?"

Everyone around the table, except for Ted, said, "Aye."

★

Polly and Yulleg were in the landing bay. The flagstone floor had been scrubbed clean leaving no sign of the accident; not a trace of the slippery liquid remained.

"Well?" said Yulleg, trying not to sound impatient. "Which portal did it go into?"

Polly spun around. There were dozens of portals. They surrounded the landing bay like open mouths. They looked more or less identical, except for the signs, but she hadn't paid attention to that particular detail when Scrum had thrown up the flash drive.

"Maybe that one—Stockholm," she said, trying to sound somewhat sure of herself. "Good luck, Yulleg. I'm going up to the great hall to get my dragon back." She paused for moment, still hoping she might be able to get the pendant for Natasha.

"Come help me look, Polly. It's probably not too far inside." Yulleg crutched over to the Stockholm portal.

"Besides, it doesn't sound like you're getting Scrum back any time soon. I thought you hated him now anyway."

Polly stayed where she was and put her hands on her hips. "Then I'm going up to tell Ms. Whitford I'm ready to go home."

"Aren't you curious about what will happen to me if I step in there?"

Polly sighed and followed him. She was just a little curious. "Are you allowed to just walk in there? I've never seen anyone do that. We're always flying. What if it just drops off, and we end up falling to the centre of the earth?"

"That's one of my favourite books, you know—*Journey to the Center of the Earth* by Jules Verne."

Polly rolled her eyes. "Who cares?"

Yulleg smiled at her, tossed his crutches aside, and lay down on the floor near the portal opening. "I'll just ease myself in—Polly, grab onto my legs, just in case you're right and it does drop off to the center of the earth."

Polly grabbed Yulleg's ankles roughly.

"Take it easy! My ankle's sprained!"

Polly relaxed her grip, and Yulleg inched forward into the portal. "The floor is still here," he called, when all but his toes were left in the landing bay. "Seems solid. I'm going to stand up. Pass me my crutches."

Polly let go and slid his crutches into the darkness. Moments passed. Polly stared after him wishing she had asked for the necklace.

Yulleg materialized unexpectedly, making Polly jump.

"In case something happens to me—not that anything will—I want you to have this." He pulled the dragon pendant out of his pocket and put it around Polly's neck. "Tell your dad I'm sorry I took it." He smiled.

Polly smiled back. Natasha would be thrilled. "Thank you. It's really good."

Yulleg grinned. "I'll be back in a minute." He disappeared into the darkness.

Polly forced herself to count to twenty before she called out, "Yulleg, are you there?"

When there was no reply, Polly called his name again. There was no reply, not a sound.

Just then, Polly's dad came into the landing bay with Xelif and Ms. Whitford.

Polly ran over to them. "Yulleg is in one of the portals. He walked in and disappeared."

Polly's dad and Ms. Whitford looked at each other. "Where is he going?" asked Ms. Whitford.

"He went looking for a flash drive. He said it was his, but he lost it, and then Scrum found it on the floor of the great hall and ate it. I made Scrum drink water, then he threw up, and it went flying into one of the portals. That was right before you crashed into Scrum."

"Do you think the flash drive has a copy of his book on it?" asked Ms. Whitford.

Ted nodded. "It might be the only copy. Yulleg deleted the original file off his laptop and took a copy as a bargaining chip. He wants his freedom. If he's gone, he won't be coming back. I'm sure of it."

"Why didn't you tell me this before, Ted?" said Ms. Whitford.

He turned to Polly asked, "Which portal is he in?"

Polly turned around and pointed. "Stockholm."

"Ted, you are not going after Yulleg," said Ms. Whitford, sharply.

"Then Polly and Scrum can go rescue him." Ted looked at Polly and winked.

"Dad...I can't," Polly mumbled. "Scrum won't see me."

"Why would you say that?" he asked, climbing on Xelif's back.

"Because...well...I decided I don't want to be a writer any more. I'm not Yulleg. I suck. I can't even figure how to finish one little story." Polly touched the pendant. Yulleg had carved tiny scales into the wood, and the texture reminded her of Scrum.

"Ted," said Ms. Whitford, "there's no time for this."

Ted gritted his teeth. "Polly—I have to go...I'm sorry...about everything." The he looked at Xelif and said, "Fly!" The dragon stretched his wings and lifted off.

Polly watched him fly through a familiar portal. "Is he going to the clinic?" she asked.

"Yes. I just hope the doctor is in," said Ms. Whitford. Then, as soon as Xelif's tail disappeared, she crossed the floor and stood in the middle of the landing bay. She raised her hands in front of her. She closed her eyes and began spinning in slow, steady circles.

Polly was frightened and took several steps toward the exit.

Ms. Whitford's hair was completely loose and whirling around her face. "Get me a pen," she croaked. "Quickly." She started to gag. Thick, clear liquid seeped out of the corners of her mouth.

Polly had nothing to write with. "I don't—wait!" She took off the dragon pendant. "What about this? Will it work?"

"Give it to me. Hurry!" said Ms. Whitford, her voice ragged and breathy.

Polly handed over the necklace, then backed away, quickly. Ms. Whitford held it out in front of her as she spun faster and faster. She was chanting now.

A low, guttural song reverberated off the walls of the landing bay.

Polly backed farther away from the spinning figure. The dervish breeze lifted her hair.

With a violent lurch, the spinning and chanting ceased. Ms. Whitford, her hair tangled and glasses askew, walked toward the Stockholm portal. "The flash drive is in here, and I think we had better try and find it."

CHAPTER SEVENTEEN

Rescue

"I'm going to...I mean we—Scrum and I—are going to Stockholm to rescue Yulleg, and we can look for the flash drive while we are there. Scrum has an amazing sense of smell, and he definitely knows what it smells like."

"No," said an exhausted-looking Ms. Whitford as she leaned on Polly's writing table with trembling hands. "You are staying here. You promised you would keep writing, and write you will."

Polly reached out with both of her hands, placed them on top of Ms. Whitford's, and squeezed them gently. "But you said Yulleg and the drive are both in the Stockholm portal."

"I know," snapped Ms. Whitford, pulling her hands away. She took a deep breath, trying to exhale some of her frustration. "But the divination," she continued, forcing her voice to have a more normal tone, "may have been corrupted. The pendant complicated matters." She nodded at the dragon hanging around Polly's neck.

Polly touched it protectively.

Ms. Whitford's voice grew edgy again. "Writers can only divine accurately with a writing instrument. Even I can't overcome that limitation. I have sent two writers to find Yulleg and twenty others to search every portal until we find the flash drive."

"But Scrum has those giant nostrils and—"

"Absolutely not! Just work! Just write! Let me close this chapter in the Guild's history, so we can move forward. No one is getting any writing done, no dragons are being trained, and—look at the monitors! Every day, there are new dragons popping out of unsuspecting, pubescent writers all over the world. We have been too busy playing detective to do what we need to do, what we all signed up to do—help young wannabe writers find their way to publication. Especially you, Polly. I've let you coast along as a champion procrastinator. You should at least have your first draft written by now. At least!"

Polly looked down at the blank worksheet that had been sitting on the table, untouched, for days. On their way up from the landing bay, she had promised Ms. Whitford she wouldn't give up on her dream of being a writer. Ms. Whitford had been pleased to hear that. But when Polly has asked to see Scrum, Ms. Whitford had forbidden it. She insisted Polly first prove herself by completing all her unfinished work.

Polly picked up the sheets of paper and tapped the edges together. "May I work in Scrum's room and keep him company?"

"You may not. You have broken my trust, Polly. You need to show me you are serious, or I won't be able to help you any more. I have been far too lenient with you, and it stops now."

Polly didn't look up when Ms. Whitford walked away.

Polly didn't know what was wrong. Deep down, she still wanted to be a writer, but on the surface she couldn't take hold of herself and settle into the work. She knew what she needed to be doing—but she couldn't do it. Her mind whirred like a printing press, and she was hopelessly distracted by everything all the time. She was stuck in wannabe-mode and could not snap out of it.

Polly picked up the timer and turned it over. White sand began pouring into the bottom bulb. Polly pulled out a sheet of blank paper. She took up a pen, a slippery one like the pen she had first used in Ms. Whitford's cozy writing room. She told herself to stop thinking: once, twice, a dozen times.

Finally, her hand started moving across the page.

She wrote random words and half-baked, messy sentences, but she did not stop, and she did not think. Polly wrote until the sand ran out. Then she flipped the timer over and did it again.

When she was thoroughly warmed up, she set aside the slippery pen, picked up a freshly sharpened white pencil, smiled at the words *Scrum Food* printed on its side, and read Ms. Whitford's instructions.

Then, without hesitation, she wrote the plot, setting, and character paragraphs; then she wrote thick descriptions of the opening scene, the climax, and the last scene. She also filled out the focusing worksheet, excited that this particular story—a true Polly story—was starting to come to life vividly in her imagination. She completed the form quickly, only backtracking once to change the title from just "Vamperwolf" to "How I Became a Vamperwolf."

> Working Title: *How I Became a Vamperwolf*
> Genre: *Teen Fiction*
> Category: *Fantasy*
> Theme: *Dreams don't come true from just dreaming*
> Audience: *Teens like me*
> Tone: *Mysterious, surprising*
> Purpose: *Show that you can't just dream— you have to do stuff*
> Point of View: *First person*
> Main Setting: *Vampire clubhouse*
> Atmosphere: *Lonely and sad at beginning*
> Hook: *First time she hears about the club*
> Protagonist: *Teen girl with a vampire obsession*

Protagonist's Need: *Be part of the vampire club*
Protagonist's Allies: *One of the girls from the club*
Protagonist's Enemies: *Her fear of being rejected*
Conflict: *Girl v. herself*
Climax: *The girl stands outside clubhouse—
will she go in?*
Ending: *Finds a silver bullet and gets magical
powers that allow her to transform into a real
vampire or a real werewolf*
Protagonist's Growth: *Girl is happy because the
outcome is even better than she imagined it could be*

Polly put her pencil down and smiled. She was eager to see Scrum, but now that her imagination was fired up, and she could see the scenes vividly on her inner movie screen, she didn't want to stop writing. She pulled out a fresh piece of paper, put her working title at the top, and let her imagination mess up the tidy blank page.

The first paragraph came out so quickly Polly could hardly keep pace with the spurt of words. The second paragraph came readily too. So did the third paragraph. The fourth paragraph was a breeze. It was the fifth that caught her.

The story begged for a setting change, and Polly couldn't think of one. In a panic, she went back to the first paragraph and started editing. The more she edited, the less she liked her story. It was bad writing and getting worse by the stroke.

Polly's pencil froze. She put it in her mouth sideways and let her teeth sink into the crunchy white paint. This made her think of Scrum. It was a good time to go visit him, but not before she talked to Ms. Whitford. Maybe she could look it over and tell her what she needed to fix.

Polly looked up. She could see Ms. Whitford on the far side of the massive hall, standing with her fists jammed into her hips. Polly picked up her unfinished manuscript, which was four paragraphs and two precious pages long, and walked across the hall and around the table to where the giant screens hung from the cave wall. She came up behind Ms. Whitford, who was talking to someone through her headset.

"Roger that. Warwickshire and Oak Park are clear. Please return to headquarters." Ms. Whitford sighed. "That's all but two left."

"Two what?" asked Polly.

Ms. Whitford turned around. Her bun had come undone again, and long tendrils of hair were falling into her eyes. Her glasses were on the bridge of her nose but slightly askew, and her cheeks were flushed.

"Two portals left and still no sign of Yulleg's flash drive. Roger that." Ms. Whitford ignored Polly.

"What about Yulleg? Did he come back? Did you find him?"

Ms. Whitford didn't answer. She was accepting a clipboard from one of the writers who was closely monitoring the "birth" of literary dragons. She read the report out loud. "We just lost sixteen emergent dragons in Los Angeles, seven in Sidney, and reports are coming in from at least ten other cities. Bangalore. Manila. London. Toronto...are you sure? This can't be happening. What do you mean they just vanished off our radar?"

Polly's mouth opened, and she spoke before she could think. "You mean they're dead when they pop out of their writers?"

Ms. Whitford shook her head. "Somehow the dragons are emerging without the writer-dragon bond in place. Without that bond, we can't track them. We can only track the bond, not the dragon or even the writer. And when a dragon leaves a writer, the writer is not a writer anymore, which is why the light goes out on the screen. This is terrible. We have no idea where the dragons are or what they are doing. All we know is twenty-three talented young writers will never be able to share their stories with the world. This is a tragedy, and I don't have any answers."

"Look!" shouted one of the writers.

Laura Michelle Thomas

Polly watched as two more lights came on and immediately winked out.

"Oh, no," whispered Ms. Whitford. The clipboard slipped out of her hands and startled everyone when it crashed to the floor. In ones and twos, lights were winking out across the map, rippling outward from heavily populated areas in China, India, Northern Europe, Central America, eastern North America, southern Mexico, and both coasts of South America.

Ms. Whitford steadied herself on Polly's shoulder. "We have to reach your father. But I can't leave head-quarters, and I need every writer who is here manning the computers to stay put. None of the other writers have returned yet. Take Scrum, find your father, and tell him to get back here with Miriam as soon as he can."

Polly looked at her unfinished manuscript. She offered it to Ms. Whitford. "I started my first draft, but I'm stuck. Can you look at it while I'm gone?"

Ms. Whitford raised her voice and said, "Never ask for feedback on an unfinished first draft! Do you under-stand me, Polly?"

Polly nodded even though she really didn't under-stand what all the fuss was about. Why couldn't she ask for feedback on her first draft? So what if it wasn't finished?

Ms. Whitford spoke harshly. "I'm dead serious. If you let your dragon, or any critic, interfere with the creative process this early on, your story will never attain its full richness and complexity. When you are writing your first draft, you must say yes to every idea, yes to every vision that pops into your imagination. They won't all be good ideas, but they will somehow enrich the final product. Just write. You're thinking too much. Just have fun!" Ms. Whitford was practically screaming at Polly. "Think about it: how can you, or I, determine if the beginning is any good if you have not even written the ending yet? How? It's much too soon to be asking for feedback."

"Masterteller," said a man walking over, his face pale. "Felix is awake. He says he has something to tell you about Johan."

Ms. Whitford raised an eyebrow, then looked at Polly. "Get Scrum. Go find your father and tell him to hurry. Go!"

Polly hurried to her desk and carefully placed her manuscript on it. She looked around for a rock or a book to hold it down, in case someone rushed by and caused a breeze that would blow it off the table. Finding none, she removed the dragon pendant and placed it on the papers. She let her fingertips linger on the dragon's broad belly and wondered what Stockholm was like at this time of year.

*

Yulleg sat with his throbbing leg on a chair in a busy café in the heart of Stockholm University campus. He sipped a cup of coffee with cream and sugar, which a young woman had bought for him right after he had signed a copy of one of his early novels, *The Adopted Son*, which she was studying in her second-year literature class. The irony irritated him now that he knew the truth, or at least some of the truth, about his parents. Yulleg had begged the young woman to keep her voice down and not draw attention to him, but her wide eyes and tremulous fingers told him he didn't have long until every girl on campus knew where he was.

He chewed the last piece of an apple tart and blew on his coffee to cool it off. His ran his thumb over the silver flash drive tucked safely in the front pocket of his jeans. He knew it wouldn't be long before either the café flooded with Yulleg Snoblivski fans or writers from the Guild found him and took him back to headquarters. He didn't intend on letting either of those things happen. This was his chance to make a fresh start and leave the writing prodigy crown behind.

When his coffee had cooled, Yulleg drained the glass mug and picked up his crutches. He had fallen badly in the dark portal. By the time he had lifted himself out of the pool, his ankle was throbbing. He suspected it was no longer just sprained but broken. Nevertheless, he gritted his teeth, hoisted himself up on his crutches, and started heading for the exit.

Yulleg stopped just short of the glass doors. Two Guild members, a man and woman, were talking to the young woman whose book he had signed. He ducked behind a bookcase.

"Bathroom?" he asked a young man sitting at a nearby table.

The young man stared at his laptop with his fists digging into his forehead and did not answer.

"Bathroom?" asked Yulleg again.

The young man looked up with a pained expression. "I've lost it. I've got nothing. My head used to be full of ideas at high school. I never took them seriously or wrote anything down; I just had this feeling inside me that I wanted to be a writer. Last night, I was so angry at myself for holding it in. And now that I've decided to start writing and let it out, it's gone. I've lost it!"

Yulleg grabbed the young man by the collar and pulled him up out of his chair. "You are going to show me where the bathroom is. Okay?"

"Yeah, sure. Take it easy," he said, leading Yulleg to a steep, narrow staircase at the back of the café. "I went to bed last night full of ideas, but this morning I don't even want to be a writer anymore. I don't even remember why I wanted to be a writer in the first place. What's happened to me?"

Yulleg hopped down the stairs behind him. "Consider yourself lucky. Take it from me, writing gets mind-numbing after a while."

When they reached the bottom of the stairs, the young man stopped and studied Yulleg. "I know you. You're—"

"No time for autographs. I need to get out of here, fast."

"Must be tough being so popular with the ladies." He winked and pointed. "That way. There's a back door."

Yulleg went down a long corridor past rows of coffee beans in wooden crates until he found a low door at the top of a narrow flight of stairs. He smiled. Freedom lay just on the other side. All he had to do was get himself into the throng of students and blend in. Then he would go to the countryside and find a job in a small Swedish town as an apprentice under the tutelage of an old-world sculptor. As for the silver flash drive, he planned to hang on to it just in case Felix or Mammozarack or anyone from Mightright came calling, grubbing for scraps in the Yulleg Snoblivski trough. If it truly held the only copy of *Dragon by a Tale*, he could use it to bargain for just about anything he might need later on.

Yulleg put his hand on the antique doorknob and turned. The door swung open. The bright light made his eyes sting.

"Hello, Mr. Snoblivski," said Polly. She stood just on the other side of the door, her knuckles jammed into her hips.

Yulleg kept his face neutral, trying to appear as if he popped out of the backside of this particular café on a regular basis. "Excuse me, please. I'm on my way. Nice to see you one last time." He used his crutches to push her out of his way. "Give my regards to your father. Tell him I enjoyed working with him."

Polly caught up with him. "You can tell him yourself. You're coming back to headquarters with me."

"I don't think so!" Yulleg charged on, pulling ahead. When he saw Polly was able to keep up, he picked up the pace and asked, "How did you know where I was?"

"Duh! There's a mob of girls in front of the café. They're organizing into queues so you can sign their body parts." Polly had to run to keep up. The cobble-stones and other pedestrians made it difficult. "Stop, Yulleg. Just stop and talk to me for a minute. I'm staying.

I decided to be a writer again, and I need…can you help me with my first draft? I'm stuck."

"No," said Yulleg. He doubled the pace and headed down an alley between the old brick buildings, away from the main flow of pedestrian traffic. Desperate to get him to stop, Polly threw her leg out and kicked his sore ankle.

He dropped like a sack of bricks to the cobblestone road.

Polly knelt down beside him as he writhed in agony. "Are you okay?" she asked.

Yulleg's face was pale. His hair was pasted to his forehead with beads of sweat. "Do I look okay?"

"Sorry, but we need to get you back to the reflecting pool and onto Scrum's back. We'll make a quick stop, and then we'll get you back to the Guild so you can rest up your ankle. When you're better you can help me with—"

"Polly," said Yulleg, wincing as she helped him sit up. "I really like you, but there is nothing left for me at the Guild. I have to disappear. I want a different life, one where I'm not an author. I'll never be free if I go back."

"But you're rich and famous. You have everything I've ever wanted."

"No. I don't." Yulleg used his crutches to get to his feet.

"Please come with me to Dr. Mammozarack's clinic. I have to give my dad a message, and I really need your help with my story. I'm totally stuck."

Yulleg adjusted his crutches. "Sorry. I don't write any more. You're on your own."

The noise of an anxious crowd rose, and someone shouted, "He went down there!"

Polly and Yulleg watched from the bushes as hundreds of girls streamed past the entry to the alley, running in the wrong direction.

"I can't believe you are going to give all this up."

"Let me give you a few pieces of advice, Miss Wannabe. One, don't think so much; just have fun

Polly Wants to Be a Writer   **159**

writing your first draft. Two, it's impossible to say how good the beginning of a story is until you have written the ending." He smiled. "And three, whatever you do, don't ask Scrum for help until you've finished the first draft. And four, I can tell you from experience that when you turn Scrum loose on your first draft, he will be brilliant. Listen to him. Dragons are amazing sculptors." Yulleg nodded. Then he took off down the alley at full tilt, swinging his crutches madly.

Polly walked back to the reflecting pool in the campus garden. Her arms were dead straight at her side, and her fists were clenched. She hoped Yulleg would be found by the mob and made to sign autographs until his fingers bled. Tears stung her eyes. It wasn't fair. Why was she the one always getting stuck? Why didn't the words just flow? Why was this so hard for her?

Polly cut the final corner, shoving her shoulder into a tall hedge. She stopped short on the garden path. By the reflecting pool, a group of dragons crowded around Scrum. Six of them, in all shapes and sizes, held him down. Another dragon, a larger black dragon, was poised over Scrum's face with his jaws open. She could see the red glow in his midsection. He was about to singe Scrum.

"Let him go!" she commanded. The dragons seemed shocked that she could see them. They momentarily relaxed their grip enough to let Scrum get his tail free. He whipped it around and knocked two of the dragons to the ground, but the others realized what was happening and tightened their grips. Scrum cried out with pain.

Polly ran a few steps closer, unsure what she could do without a weapon. Then she noticed the path around the pool was made of loose stones. She bent down, picked up a handful, and starting pitching them at the dragons. She hit Scrum almost as many times as she hit the others, but when she hit the black dragon in the eye, he took off. The rest of the gang let go of Scrum, and followed the ringleader into the bushes.

Polly jumped on Scrum's pale back and said, "Fly!"
With effort, Scrum lifted off.

"I didn't know the other dragons were bullying you that badly. Why didn't you tell me?" Polly felt the wind grow stronger on her face. Her hair whipped behind her like a flag. Looking down at the campus grounds, the reflecting pool seemed like a tiny rectangle. Two Guild writers and their dragons were just emerging from the garden.

"Those weren't Guild dragons. They've never heard of the Guild, and they don't have writers."

Polly remembered the lights winking out on the big screens. These were the young dragons who had popped out of their writers without a writer-dragon bond. But how could there be so many? Her stomach clenched as Scrum hovered midair and began to turn his nose down for the dive.

Just before they hit the surface of the portal, Polly saw the pack of rogue dragons burst out of the bushes and attack the two writers from the Guild.

Polly crouched down low on Scrum's back and wrapped her arms tightly around his long neck as they tore through the portal.

"We need to find my dad! To the clinic! Hurry!"

Scrum heard but didn't reply. He spread his wings wide to brake. They sailed into the landing bay, flew around the dome once, and then rocketed into the portal leading to Dr. Mammozarack's depression clinic for teen girls.

CHAPTER EIGHTEEN

Quill

Polly and Scrum were in the reflecting pool in the courtyard at Dr. Mammozarack's clinic. It was warm, and the air was thick and sweet with pollen. Polly shivered. She did not feel good about being back.

She nodded at Scrum and began to crawl stealthily out of the pool. Polly stayed on her stomach and wormed her way across the concrete toward the door. Scrum followed, staying low, close on her heels.

At the door, Polly stood up and pressed her back into the cool concrete wall. Scrum crouched down and unfurled his long body along the wall beside hers.

"Scrum?" she whispered, her voice quavering.

Scrum looked at her and blinked.

"I don't know what we're going to do when we get inside. How are we going to find my dad in that place?" She recalled the maze of hallways and did not like the thought of going around in circles again. "I wish there was another way inside."

Scrum lifted up his bearded chin and looked at the patch of sky above them. "Let's find out."

Polly looked up. "Good thinking, Scrum," she whispered as she slipped onto his back.

Scrum flew dozens of floors up from the courtyard and shot through the opening between the buildings.

Polly drew in her breath. The clinic, which from the street looked like an ordinary two-story office building, was not. The side of the building overlooking the courtyard, and the courtyard itself, was deep underground. Only the top two floors were above ground.

"Look, on the roof!" said Polly. "It looks like a reflecting pool. It must be a way in."

Scrum climbed higher and then began to dive.

As they plummeted, Polly noticed something strange about their reflection in the pool's surface. Scrum's image was crystal clear, and there were no ripples on the surface.

"It's a mirror!" she yelled. "Stop! Pull up!"

But it was too late for Scrum to pull up.

Polly braced herself for the pain of being sliced as they crashed through the mirror, but when Scrum hit the glass, nothing shattered. They flew right inside the top floor of the building, unharmed.

Scrum landed, and Polly once again drew in her breath. "What is this place?" she whispered.

In the middle of the cavernous room, in the middle of a wide moat, sat a steel sphere three-times Polly's height. Scrum walked to the edge of the moat and looked across at the bizarre, polished ball. Electric sparks flickered along the surface of the thick blue liquid that oozed inside the moat. There didn't seem to be any way across.

Polly searched the room for an exit. "Looks dangerous. Let's go find my dad."

"Hello, hello, hello," said a high-pitched, female voice.

Scrum stopped. "Polly, was that you?"

"No."

Polly said loudly, "Where are you?"

"In here, in here, in here," sang the voice. "Do you have a treat for me—a sweet treat to eat?"

Polly and Scrum looked at the steel sphere and then at each other.

"Can you fly over the moat and land on top of it?"

Scrum nodded and flew across the moat.

"There's a window!" said Polly, looking down.

Scrum hovered over the window. Polly looked inside. She couldn't see anything. "Land, Scrum."

The sphere was so big Scrum had ample room to land.

Polly slid off his back and peered inside. "Do you see anyone in there?" she asked.

A pale pink figure darted in and out of view.

"If you don't have a sweat treat to eat, you can go, go, go away. I don't like strangers." The voiced echoed all around them, girlish and pouty.

"I think it's a dragon," Polly said, "not a person."

Scrum furrowed his bony eyebrows and took on an air of authority. "Who put you in there?"

A figure came into view. It was a light pink dragon with over-sized wings. She was smaller than Scrum but had the same oversized nostrils.

"You are a stranger and ugly too," she teased. "Ugly-puggly."

Scrum frowned and snorted. "Why are you in there? Answer me or I will...I will..."

The dragon giggled. "Nice to meet you, I-will-I-will."

Polly stifled a laugh. The dragon was terribly cute. She was mostly face and wings, wings so big for her little frame they didn't stay in place, even when folded.

Scrum was clearly flustered. "Why you pink ball of—"

"Sh," said Polly, putting her hand on Scrum's trembling side. "Be gentle with her. Poor thing. Who put your in there?" Polly asked the little pink dragon.

"My writer."

"Did you do something bad?"

The dragon nodded with mock sadness. "I've been a bad-sad-mad dragon."

"What is your writer's name?" asked Polly.

"Mo-mo-mo."

"I've never heard of him," said Scrum. "Is he famous?"

"She's a she; she's not a he," giggled the dragon.

Polly leaned over to Scrum's ear and whispered, "I think she's talking about Miriam Mammozarack, but she must be confused. Yulleg told me the doctor's dragon is already dead."

Scrum looked surprised. "The doctor's dragon is named Quill, and she's not dead. I'm sure of it. This could be her."

Polly shook her head. "I'm sure Quill is dead. Yulleg said Mammozarack killed her and then blamed Felix for it. Yulleg got the story from Felix, who loved Quill. I think Yulleg must know the truth. This can't be her."

Scrum looked puzzled. "Some of the dragons know about Quill from the old days. They say she was untrainable and allergic to everything, but they never said she was dead or spoke about her in the past tense."

Polly looked at Scrum. "I don't think this is Quill."

Scrum frowned and whispered forcefully, "I think it is her."

"Are you a writer?" asked the dragon, looking up at Polly. "Only a writer can set me free."

Polly looked at Scrum and fumbled for the right words. "Sort of...maybe."

"That's too bad," said the dragon. "I would really like to go outside and see what it's like out there. My friend and I almost went outside once. That was a sad-mad-bad day. My friend got a big ouch and went ugly-puggly, but I still love him. He is my special friend. I bliss-kiss-miss my Felix-welix."

"You've never been outside?" said Scrum.

"Felix is your special friend?" said Polly at the same time.

"Never and, yes, he is," said the dragon.

Scrum stared at Polly. Polly stared at Scrum. Then they both looked through the window at the dragon. It was Quill. Somehow she was alive. Quill looked up at them and blinked.

Scrum lowered his head to the glass and said, "Polly is a writer—a real one. Tell her what she needs to do to get you out of there."

Quill grinned. "You have to say: I wish you were out."

"Is that it?" asked Polly.

"Yes. Please hurry. I really want to get out, and if Mo-mo comes we will be punished for being bad. She might even put a thingy in your forehead."

"What thingy?" asked Polly.

"Just a mini, metal bit and bob. She says I'm very badly allergic to them, that's why I have to stay in here and never go outside. Please let me out, please, before she comes and you get a whatchamacallit in your head."

Polly looked down at the pitiful, pink face and said, "I wish you were out."

Gears squealed into motion, and the steel ball immediately began to open like a blooming flower. Scrum had to flap his wings to avoid falling on Quill.

When the ball was completely open, the steel petals lay across the moat like bridges. Quill half-walked, half-danced her way across one of the petals. She hummed as she went, her wings waving behind her like flags.

Scrum landed next to her.

"Thank you!" sang Quill. She held the last note as long as she could. With her next breath, she asked Scrum if he knew any dragon songs or sky games.

Scrum shook his head and shrugged.

"She looks a lot like you, Scrum," said Polly, noting the snake-like body and mottled pinky-white scales. "It's like you come from the same family. Maybe you're cousins or something."

"Cousins?" said the dragons in concert.

"Is your name Will?" asked Quill. She looked up at Scrum with a mildly irritating mixture of admiration and haughtiness.

"My name is Scrum."

"Scrum," Quill giggled. "That's a weird name for a dragon."

Polly couldn't help giggling and adding, "He is weird."

Scrum frowned at her.

Polly smiled and said, "Do you know the way out, Quill?"

"Follow me-lee-lee."

★

Ms. Whitford was in a dark room similar, yet bigger and emptier, than the one she had used to question Polly's father. She wore her special glasses, the ones that let her see the tiny dragon balled up in a corner.

She spoke into the dark silence, "We're in trouble, Felix."

Felix jumped at the sound of Ms. Whitford's voice.

"We've lost hundreds of emergent literary dragons in the last hour alone. They popped out and, immediately, vanished from our radar. Think of it: hundreds of potential writers with no dragons to help them become professionals—what can you tell me about this?"

Felix was obviously shocked. "Nothing...I...maybe it's an equipment malfunction. Your radar might have been damaged. Maybe Miriam sabotaged it."

"I don't think so. There was an incident in Stockholm I need explained."

Felix looked even more confused.

"Two writers were found by the portal, badly injured. They were attacked by a gang of these rogue dragons."

Felix's eyes were wide in the dark. The nub of his tail and the stumps of his wings twitched. "I swear. I don't know anything about missing dragons or gangs of rogues."

Ms. Whitford sat down on the stone floor next to Felix. She put her hand out and stroked his back. "Never mind that now. Let's talk about you and Quill."

Felix smiled and relaxed as Ms. Whitford continued stroking his back.

"Miriam used you to replace Quill, didn't she?" she asked.

Felix nodded. "Quill was too clever for her."

"Can you tell me what happened the day Johan died? What did you see?"

Felix bowed his head. "I loved her so much."

"I know. Please tell me about that day."

Felix sniffed. "Miriam always kept her locked up... in terrible contraptions. Quill always got out, but then Miriam would find her and...I can't talk about that part." Felix let out a sob. "Whenever Johan went to Miriam's laboratory, they let me keep Quill company. I used to sit beside her cage, with my body right up against hers as best I could, and tell her about the world outside. She loved my stories, and she always asked me to describe the world. She begged me to find the right words. She wanted to see the world with all senses. When I found just the right adjectives and nouns and verbs, she would cry. She was so sensitive."

Ms. Whitford smiled. "I'm sure this is why you became such an exceptional partner for Yulleg. All that thick, vivid, sensory description you found for Quill, it was great practice for you."

At the mention of Yulleg's name, Felix perked up slightly. "He's a good boy. We made magic together. I never meant to lose him...but I suppose I have."

"We don't know where he is, Felix. It appears he has run away."

"This is the end, then. I have lost everyone I care about. And now *Dragon by a Tale* won't be released, and Quill's story will never be told. This is the end."

"Felix, this is not the end. You can help me save other young writers. Tell me what happened the day Johan died," urged Ms. Whitford, "the whole story."

Felix licked his lips, took a shallow breath, and began. "It was summer. When I arrived at Miriam's lab with Johan, I was excited to tell Quill about a hummingbird I had just about flown into on the way to see her. I knew she would love to hear about how tiny a hummingbird is, and how it vibrates when it flies in its zig-zag way. But when we got there, Quill wasn't in her cage. She was strapped to a table." Felix paused, unable to continue.

Ms. Whitford picked Felix up and put him on her lap. She wrapped both arms around him. "Go on. You can tell me. I want to hear Quill's story."

★

Polly's dad and Dr. Miriam Mammozarack walked down a narrow corridor. Xelif followed slowly, his wide frame making it difficult to keep up.

The doctor was smiling. "Over nine thousand dragons have been put under my control as of the latest report."

Ted whistled, pretending to sound impressed and unconcerned at the same time. "You still have a long way to go before every dragon on the planet is yours."

"True, but I am confident my team of rogues will complete their task within just a few hours."

"How is that possible?"

"You will see," she said, placing an antique calligraphy pen into a book-shaped lock by a door in the hallway. "By the way, Ted, you can stop asking me to come back to the Guild. I am not a member. They have no hold over me," she snickered. "That bond is entirely broken." She brushed away a stringy lock of hair that had fallen over her pinched face.

A door slid open.

Ted glanced back to see if Xelif was still following them, but he wasn't. He had no choice but to follow Dr. Mammozarack into what appeared to be a control room.

The door slid shut behind them.

Inside, an image of an open book was being projected onto a plain, white wall making a large screen. The image ran from floor to ceiling and from one corner of the room to the other. On it, thousands of TV-shaped video images dotted the open pages. The doctor walked over to the wall. The back of her laboratory coat was illuminated by the light of the projector as she pointed to the icons. "I can track all my dragons from here. This is what each one of them is seeing right now."

"Amazing," said Ted, his mouth open. "How?"

"So simple."

The doctor pulled a strange looking gun out of her pocket, walked up to Ted, and jammed the muzzle into his forehead. Before he could react, she pulled the trigger.

Ted didn't feel any pain, but he could feel something lodged deep inside his forehead.

Dr. Mammozarack went over to a computer and selected one of the images. She clicked on it. "Look at the screen now," she said.

Ted looked up. One of the icons was now open as a full window, and inside was exactly the same view that he was seeing. When Ted turned his head and looked at the doctor, the view changed to that image. "You put a camera in my forehead? I don't get it."

"It's far more than a camera, Ted. I can hear everything too. And the sound and the images are coming from your brain, not from a camera or a microphone. So simple. All I had to do was tap into the part of your frontal lobe controlling the dragon-writer bond. A little something I threw together while the rest of you were off writing love poems. Felix was my first successful test subject, and it worked just fine too, until the boy started scribbling, then something about Felix's old bond with Johan overcame the implanted bond. And the ugly, little dragon left me, just like Johan did."

Ted clenched his teeth. "Yulleg is your boy, isn't he?"

"Of course he is. Are you Guild writers always so dense? Doesn't it make sense that I would be the mother of the greatest literary genius in history?"

Ted's fists clenched, and his head grew hot. But he kept his voice light, reminding himself that he was supposed to be bringing her back to the Guild for questioning unharmed. "Of course. Any child of yours and Johan would be gifted. I didn't mean to be rude."

"I don't like your tone, Ted. It reminds me that sixteen years ago you refused an invitation because you had...a better offer." She put two fingers to a scale-shaped, metal pendant hanging around her neck and sang one word: "nemesis."

An electric shock exploded in Ted's frontal lobe and tore through his body. His knees buckled, and he fell to the floor. "Stop...please," he gasped.

The shock stopped, leaving Ted on all fours, panting, trying to regain his senses. He shook his head to clear his vision and looked up to where the doctor stood by her desk. There was a silver urn beside the computer monitor. "This is what you did to Quill. This is how you killed her, isn't it? You tortured her to death."

The doctor's eyes narrowed. "My implant might not control human behaviour like it does with dragons, however, the functions that control pain and death work just as well in both species. And the implant does make a lovely sound when it explodes." A wry smile crossed her face. "Watch this."

Ted looked up at the screen. The doctor minimized the window with Ted's view in it and selected another video, one that was completely black.

Ted recognized Felix's voice immediately.

The dragon was speaking, his voice full of raw emotion. "...she was strapped to a table, and then Miriam put a gun against her forehead and pulled the trigger, and this thing went under her skin, but then it popped right out again. Miriam tried shooting it in over and over, but it wouldn't stay in, so Johan said she could try it on me. He told me to stand still, and I did. I trusted him. She shot something into my forehead, and it stayed there.

"Right away, I felt my bond with Johan start to fade and a new bond with Miriam start to take over. When Johan sensed it, he begged her to take it out of me, but she refused. They fought, and Quill and I ran out of the laboratory. We were just about to go outside when... it...when I...changed." Felix inhaled stiffly. "When Quill brought me back to the laboratory to get help for my burns, Johan was dead. I should have died too that day. I don't know what happened..." Felix broke down, sobbing.

"I knew it was you!" Ted growled. He was on his feet now, swaying from the aftereffects of the shock. All thoughts of bringing Miriam back to the Guild "unharmed" were gone.

Miriam sneered at Ted. "Sh," she said, "this is getting good."

Felix was speaking again, his voice broken with sadness. "But I didn't die. I was changed, and the thing was still stuck in my head, and I became Miriam's dragon. I was there the day Yulleg was born and the day she gave him up for adoption. My bond with Miriam was strong, but not perfect. What truly kept me with her was seeing Quill every day. But the first time Yulleg picked up a crayon and wrote a letter, something changed. The thing in my head grew weaker, and I needed to be with Yulleg. I knew I had to leave the clinic, but I couldn't go without my Quill. I tried to escape with her, but Miriam caught us. Quill convinced her to let me go, but she had to stay behind." Felix voice shook with sobs again.

Ms. Whitford's voice broke in loudly. Ted could tell she must be sitting or standing very close to Felix. "Go on. Tell me everything you know. You will be helping other dragons like Quill."

"I never saw Quill again," said Felix. "When Miriam found us a few years ago, I thought I would get to see her again, but I didn't. It was too late. Miriam said she was already in her urn, and it was my fault. She told me Quill died of a broken heart just after I left the clinic to be with Yulleg. She said if I didn't let her be part of Yulleg's success she would..."

"Poor, sad, little dragon," said the doctor, her fingers drifting up to the metal pendant around her neck.

"Don't!" said Ted. "No!"

The doctor put two fingers on the pendant and sang, "The end."

Ted heard an explosion, a scream cut short, and then white noise. "You killed them!" he yelled, as he jumped on the doctor, knocked her to the floor, and wrapped his hands around her throat.

Xelif crashed through the door.

"Hello, Mo!" said Quill, smiling.

"Dad!" cried Polly. "Stop! What are you doing?"

Polly ran over to her dad, who was sitting on top of Dr. Mammozarack with his hands locked around her neck. The doctor was barely breathing, and her face was going blue and blotchy.

"Dad! Dad!" Polly tried to shake his arms loose, but they wouldn't budge. "Stop! You're killing her!"

"She killed them all. Felix is dead...and...Patti." Ted's eyes were glazed with fury. "She must be stopped."

"Ms. Whitford?" said Polly weakly. "Are you sure? I just left her to come and tell you something—Please don't do this, dad. Please. Ms. Whitford wouldn't want this—you're a writer not a fighter. Xelif! Help!"

Xelif didn't move. He wrapped his thick tail around Scrum to stop him from interfering.

Quill stood stone-still. "Felix. Dead? My Felix—dead?" she murmured over and over.

"Dad. Please," said Polly. "Look. Quill is alive."

Ted's jaw quivered as he forced himself to let go of the doctor's neck. Where his hands had been, purple, finger-shaped welts rose and spread. He took a deep, shaky breath, then reached down and ripped the necklace from around the doctor's neck. Then, not bothering to find out if she was still breathing, he stood up and staggered over to a chair. He sat down heavily.

Polly checked the doctor's pulse. Her heart was still beating. "She's alive, Dad. I'm so glad. If she dies, Quill will, too."

Quill broke her meditative chant and spoke to Xelif. "Your writer has a thingy in his forehead. I can take your pain away."

"Quill?" said Ted, staring at the pink dragon. "Miriam said you were dead. Your urn is right there." He pointed at the silver urn on the doctor's desk.

"Mo is a bad writer. Bad, sad, and mad."

Everyone looked at the doctor lying unconscious on the floor, while Quill walked up to Ted and licked his forehead.

"Quill! No!" said Ted.

"I can take your pain away."

"Okay. Please." Ted leaned his head forward.

Quill wriggled her claws and said, "One, two, three, snippety-snap, and out comes the whatchamacall—"

"Ouch! Thank you," he said, sitting back in the chair and putting the necklace on.

"What's that thing, Dad?"

Ted handed her the scale-like piece of metal. She was surprised by how heavy it was.

She handed it back to her dad.

"The freshly emergent dragons are being injected with implants by a special group of dragons I suspect belong to the young writers she has locked up in this place. Miriam uses musical words and this pendant to control them. We'll take her back to the Guild, and when she wakes up, we will get her to bring them all in so we can take the implants out and get them to bond with their writers."

"What about the girls? We can't just leave them. I did what Ms. Whitford said, and now I want to help them." Polly's face fell, and her lips tembled. She went to her dad and put her arms around his neck. "I can't believe she's gone."

Ted lifted Polly's arms up and made her stand up straight. "Scrum, Polly has some girls to rescue, and I want you to help her."

"Yes, Sir," said Scrum. "For Ms. Whitford."

"Yes, Sir," said Quill. "For my Felix-welix."

Ted continued. "I'm going to rig the building to implode and seal up the portal in the courtyard permanently, but I'll give you plenty of time to get them out safely and yourselves too."

"Outside?" said Quill, bouncing up and down with excitement.

"The explosion will be triggered by the next creature who passes through the portal after Xelif and I. Do you understand?"

Polly, Scrum, and Quill nodded in unison.

CHAPTER NINETEEN

Empty Glass

Polly and Scrum followed Quill down an empty corridor. Polly had the feeling they were in a maze and would end up going in circles like they had last time.

"Are you sure you know the way, Quill?" asked Polly. She searched for any distinguishing features on the walls and ceiling, but there were none—just perfectly stark, white walls, a glassy black floor, and fluorescent lights overhead. They passed several closed doors, but they seemed to be evenly spaced and absolutely identical to one another.

"Yes, yes, yes," sang Quill as she skipped along. "I know where she keeps them girls-pearls-curls."

Quill disappeared around another corner and then another. Polly and Scrum doubled their pace to keep up with the bouncing pink dragon.

"Quill!" shouted Polly when they had lost sight of her for the third time.

Quill came up behind them, startling them both. "Be quietly quiet. Them girls are in here."

Polly followed Quill to a closed door that looked just the same as all the others. Quill looked at her and nodded enthusiastically. Polly turned the handle and peered inside.

It was a spacious lounge, not unlike the kind you might find in a university dormitory. Panicked, Polly quickly closed the door.

Both dragons looked at her quizzically.

"Nurses," she whispered. "There are at least twenty of them in there. These are the wrong them, Quill. We want to rescue the girls, girls like me."

Quill cocked her head, puzzled.

Polly couldn't tell if the confusion was feigned or real.

"Those are girls."

"Yes...but...no...those are women. We need to save the girls who are my age, teenagers. Do you know where they are, Quill?"

Quill scrunched up her face, flared her over-sized nostrils, and puffed open her wings as she concentrated. Polly and Scrum watched her intently.

"Mo's room! Mo's room!" shouted Quill.

"Quiet," said Polly, placing her hand on the bridge of Quill's snout to calm her down.

Quill lowered her voice to a barely audible whisper. "They are Mo's pets. She keeps them in an empty glass. Empty place, empty space. Not nice for them."

Polly didn't have time to ask Quill to explain what she meant by the empty glass, so she simply asked, "Where is Mo's room?"

"Follow me-lee-lee!" said Quill, leaping with joy right into Scrum's side.

Annoyed, Scrum whacked her hard with his tail. She landed with a loud thud against the wall and scrambled right back to her feet.

"That's was fun, Scrum! That's an imperfect rhyme but still a rhyme! Let's do it again."

The door to the nurse's lounge burst open.

"Run!" shouted Polly.

"Fun! Run!" giggled Quill.

One of the nurses shouted, "It's that wannabe! Her white dragon, too! Get them! The doctor wants to put an implant in him."

Polly, Scrum, and Quill pounded down the hallway, which was much too tight for flying. "Faster!" shouted Polly as they blindly rounded a corner. Polly had no idea where the hallway was leading them. Looking over her shoulder, Polly saw at least a dozen nurses in pale pink uniforms pour after them. Oddly, she noticed, their uniforms were the same tone of pink as Quill's skin. Polly looked at the little dragon. "Quill! We need someplace to hide."

Quill lightly bounced along. "Two rights and two rights more and down we go."

Polly was started to feel winded as she counted the rights and worried they were going to end up right back at the door to the nurses' lounge.

"Here, here, here," said Quill, stopping suddenly.

Polly and Scrum stopped. Polly couldn't see anywhere they could hide. "Quill, they are going to catch us."

Quill giggled. "No silly, they are going to catch me-me-me!" And, with that, she sang one word: "foreshadow," and a door slid open.

Before they could speak, Quill head-butted Polly and Scrum inside.

When they turned around, they caught a glimpse of Quill waving goodbye as the door blinked shut.

They were inside a lavishly appointed bedroom filled with antiques, draperies, wall-to-wall bookshelves, and a grand four-poster bed covered with layers of indigo silk and white and gold velvet that looked like it had never been slept in.

"I wish my bedroom looked like this," said Polly. She ran her fingers along the spines of the books, realizing they were multiple copies of Yulleg's novels. "Wow," she said. "The whole collection."

Scrum stood where the door had been. "What will they do to her?"

Polly walked over and tried to find a handle. She shook her head. "There doesn't seem to be a way out of here."

She felt exhausted all of a sudden, and the plush bed begged her to lie down. Polly went over to it and sat down on the indigo duvet, thinking it would be okay if she rested for just a moment or two.

She sat down tentatively. Something hard was under the covers.

"What's this?" said Polly as she got up and pulled back the duvet. It was her grandmother's antique mirror. "The girls..." said Polly, touching the glass thoughtfully.

"Scrum, when you were in the mirror that day, you said it was dark and empty. Remember what Quill said about the doctor keeping the girls in an empty glass?"

Scrum nodded at Polly, then turned away. He looked longingly at the place in the wall where the door had been.

"Right." Polly exhaled, letting out all her breath. "I'm going in there."

"Where?" said Scrum, not really paying attention.

"Inside the mirror."

"Okay," said Scrum.

Polly walked over to the bookshelf, pulled a handful of books off one of the shelves, and wedged the mirror into the empty space she had just made. She wiggled it to make sure it was secure, then crossed to the other side of the room.

She took a deep breath and started to run.

When she was two body-lengths away, she sprang and put her arms out front as if she was diving into a pool. She tucked in her chin and aimed her fingertips directly at the centre of the glass.

Polly crashed into Scrum's chest and landed on the floor hard. The index finger on her right hand—her writing hand—felt odd and tingly. When she looked up, Scrum was standing between her and the mirror.

Scrum held out his tail and offered it to Polly. She took hold of it and got back up on her feet.

"I'll go," he said.

But before he could get a run at the mirror, they heard the sound of muffled shouting coming from the hallway.

"Doctor's bedroom—blast—wall!" was all they could hear, but it was enough to know they had to find a way out, fast. The nurses had found them.

Polly hopped up on Scrum's back. "Go, Scrum!"

Just as the wall exploded and the nurses piled into the bedroom, the tip of Scrum's tail slipped beneath the surface of the glass.

In the darkness, Scrum crashed headfirst. throwing Polly off his back. She landed face down on a cold floor. Her index finger throbbed. She winced when she tried to use her right hand to sit up.

The darkness was filled with murmurs and whispers, but Polly couldn't tell which direction they were coming from. "Scrum!" she called. "Are you okay? Where are you?"

"Is that you, Polly?"

Polly hesitated at the sound of a familiar voice. "Natasha? Is that you?"

"Yes! Oh my goodness." Natasha's voice was full of relief. "What are you doing here?"

Staying on all fours, Polly crawled, carefully, to where she thought Natasha was. When she found her, the girls hugged each other fiercely.

"How many of you are there?" asked Polly.

"About thirty of us," said Natasha, squeezing her hand.

"Ouch!" said Polly.

"Are you okay?"

"I'm fine...well...one of my fingers hurts. But I'll be okay."

"I heard you were here. Some of the girls saw you in the dining hall a few days ago. Is that white dragon with you? They say he's amazing!"

The noise in the room grew louder as the rest of the girls chattered excitedly.

Laura Michelle Thomas

"Can't you smell him?" she asked Natasha. Then she called out into the darkness, "Scrum?"

"He's over here!" said one of the girls.

Polly and Natasha crawled over to where Scrum lay unconscious. Polly could feel his scaly ribcage rising and falling peacefully. "He must have hit his head when we landed. We're stuck here until he wakes up."

Polly leaned against Scrum's side. "How did you end up here?" she asked Natasha.

"Right after you and Yulleg disappeared from school, my parents got a call from Dr. Mammozarack. She said I won a writing contest I entered last year, and the prize was a week-long stay in her special training clinic for gifted writers. As soon as my parents dropped me off, I knew something was wrong. I kept asking if I could call my parents to come and get me but—"

"That's it!" said Polly. "We'll go to the reception area and call your parents. They'll come and pick you up, and you'll be safe. Once we get out of this awful place," she added, nudging Scrum. "Wake up!"

Scrum snored heavily.

"You're so lucky to have a dragon. You must be a great writer," said Natasha.

"You have a dragon too. I'm sure of it."

"I've never seen a dragon. None of us have, except for the girls who were lucky enough to see Scrum."

Polly thought about the gang of rogue dragons in Stockholm. "Maybe that's for the best right now, but my dad is at Guild headquarters and—"

"What? I thought your dad sold tractors. He's a writer?"

Before Polly could answer, Scrum sputtered and spat and sat up. "Where? What? Polly?"

"We're in the mirror. We're okay." Polly slid up on his back. "Make your body as long as you can. Hurry."

As Scrum uncoiled himself, his cold scales brushed against some of the girls. They squealed and moved quickly out of his way.

"Natasha, tell the girls to climb on, hang on, and be quiet."

Natasha organized the girls then climbed up behind Polly. She wrapped her arms tightly around Polly's waist.

"Let's go, Scrum!" shouted Polly. She tried to hold on with both hands, but her finger—the one she knew was probably broken—throbbed painfully, so she could only hold on with one. She stuck her injured hand in the crook of her arm pit. The pressure felt good.

As Scrum lifted off the ground, slowly at first under the unfamiliar weight, the girls shrieked and dug their fingernails into one another so they wouldn't fall off. Up ahead, Polly was relieved to see a point of light that was rapidly growing bigger.

"Close your eyes everyone! It's going to be bright out there!" To Scrum she said quietly, "Let's just hope the nurses are gone."

Polly closed her eyes and ducked.

When she opened them again, she was lying on Dr. Mammozarack's sumptuous bed beneath a crushing pile of sharp elbows and bony kneecaps.

"Now what?" Natasha said, straightening her clothes and smoothing out her hair. She was squinting so hard from the light, her eyes looked like they were completely closed.

Polly smiled, hiding the pain in her finger. "We need to get everyone to the reception area where the phone is and get your parents to pick you up. Then Scrum and I have to go to Guild headquarters. And listen—none of you can come back once you walk out the front door. My dad has rigged the building to implode as soon as Scrum and I leave. You know the way, right?"

"I think so," said Natasha. "Girls, this is Polly. She's a writer, and she's going to help us get home."

A cheer erupted.

"Quietly," said Polly, raising her good hand to silence the girls.

They dropped their voices to a whisper and said, "Hooray!"

　　　　　Laura Michelle Thomas

As the girls filed through the hole in the wall after Natasha, Polly looked at her grandmother's antique mirror where it was still wedged between the books. Though it had once been a doorway to Scrum's cave, it was now just a pathway to darkness and emptiness, and with Ms. Whitford gone, Polly felt enough darkness and emptiness to last a lifetime. As she picked it up off the shelf, she examined her face. The hole in the glass made it look like Polly had a third eye. It reminded her of the implant Quill had extracted from her dad's forehead.

As the last girl slipped through the hole in the wall, Scrum followed, leaving Polly alone.

She took one last look at the mirror, hefted it in her good hand, and threw it as hard as she could across the room. It smashed into one of the thick pillars of the bed frame and shattered. Splinters of white-stained wood and silver glass rained down on the inky silk bedding. Satisfied, she stuffed her bad hand into her armpit and followed Scrum into the hallway.

Polly was relieved she didn't have to lead the group. She and Natasha had been friends since kindergarten, and she trusted her completely, like a sister. She felt bad she hadn't told her about Scrum right from the beginning. She wondered what Natasha's dragon looked like and if she would be reunited with her dragon someday. Polly hoped so.

The procession stopped suddenly, and Polly walked into Scrum. She pushed her way through the crowd of girls to where Natasha was already on the phone, her voice calm.

One by one, the girls were picked up by parents who were thrilled to see their daughters but oblivious to the ordeal they had survived. Polly promised to send word to each of the girls through Natasha once she knew what was happening with their dragons.

They all said goodbye and thank you to Scrum as they left, kissing his ugly face and throwing their arms around his bony neck.

When it was just Natasha who remained, the girls hugged.

"I want to come with you to the Guild, Polly."

"I want you to come too, but the girls need you. And your parents will be here in a minute."

"What if we never get our dragons back?"

"You'll have to find a new way to become writers. Ms. Whitford..." Polly inhaled against the tears that were coming, "told me the world needs lots of writers who all write from their unique points of view. It keeps the world healthy and sane. Dragons or no dragons, we have to make sure that happens."

"Okay," said Natasha, and they hugged again. "My mom's here."

"What are you going to tell her?" asked Polly.

"I don't know. What did you tell your mom?" asked Natasha.

Polly shrugged. "I didn't know what to tell her. It's like she sees a different reality than I do. She can't even see Scrum. Only writers can, that's how I know you're a writer and that your dragon is out there somewhere."

"Oh. Then I guess I'll tell my mom I still really want to be a writer, even more now after all this. But I won't tell her about literary dragons, not yet anyway. I don't want to jinx it. I would really love to meet my dragon. Though I hope he or she doesn't smell like Scrum."

Scrum looked over at the girls and flared his nostrils at them.

Polly laughed and hugged her friend again. She would definitely give Yulleg's dragon pendant to Natasha when she got home.

"I can't believe your dad's a writer."

"Me neither."

Wishing she could go with her, Polly waved as Natasha slipped out the door.

CHAPTER TWENTY

Dragon Party

When the door clicked shut behind Natasha, Polly looked at Scrum. "We need to get out of here—fast."

"Why is your hand in your armpit? Did you hurt it?"

"Never mind. I'm fine," Polly snapped.

Scrum looked at her and blinked.

"Sorry, Scrum. I really want to go. There's something I need to do."

"What about Quill? We can't just leave her here."

"But I don't know where—"

"Where? Here?" said Quill, bouncing into the reception room, her wings more askew than normal.

"Quill!" said Scrum. He went over and put his giant nostrils up against her own. "We thought the nurses got you."

"Can't catch me! I wanna go outside."

Polly smiled. It eased the pit in her stomach a little to see Quill alive and well. She stroked the dragon's mottled pink and white back. "You're going to fly outside, Quill. But you need to help us find the courtyard first."

"Down, down, down we go!" giggled Quill.

Quill and Scrum walked side by side down the long, stark hallways until they reached the dining hall. As they walked through the room, Polly took one last look at the glass table, remembering how the nurses had wiped tears off the faces of the girls who were being shocked. She truly hoped their dragons would be found and was very glad the clinic would soon be nothing more than concrete rubble.

Polly was relieved when they finally reached the courtyard. Outside, it was bright and warm.

Quill inhaled deeply, and then without saying anything, she shot straight up like a rocket between the buildings.

"Catch her, Scrum!" yelled Polly. "She doesn't know where we're going, and if she dives through the portal before we do, we might be caught on the wrong side of the explosion."

But the little dragon with the extra-large wings was as quick as a hummingbird, and Scrum couldn't catch her. She shot up high over the rooftop, headed into the clouds, and disappeared.

Scrum launched himself upward, faster than Polly expected. She almost fell, her sore finger making it impossible to hang on with more than one hand.

They tore in and out of puffy white clouds, trying to catch sight of Quill.

"There she is," shouted Polly.

Quill had just popped out of a cloud.

Scrum banked sharply and chased the pink dragon in and around and under and through the clouds until they were finally flying side by side. Scrum pleaded with her to follow him down to the reflecting pool, but she would not listen.

"She's gone crazy, Polly. You're going to have to ride her in."

"What? I can't!" sputtered Polly, who was already struggling to hold on to Scrum. "I can't control her."

"You can control me," said Scrum, looking back at Polly with one eyebrow raised, "and I'm not exactly easy."

The dragons whirled and pitched and zigzagged through the sky. Polly knew it would be impossible to get on Quill's back, but Scrum was determined. When he managed to fly right up above Quill, he told Polly to jump.

Polly looked down at the undulating pink back and the ground scrolling along below them like a movie in fast-forward. She didn't want to do it, but they probably wouldn't get another chance like this.

Polly held her breath and jumped. She landed stomach- first on Quill's back. She kept low, wrapped her arms around the dragon's neck, and grasped her right wrist with her left hand to keep her finger from getting banged around.

"Just get her to follow me," said Scrum, taking the lead.

"Hey, Will-I-will! This is my parade!" said Quill. She lurched upward and barrel rolled over Scrum, passing him easily.

Polly squeezed her elbows deep into the sides of Quill's neck to hang on.

"Ow!" said Quill, trying to shake Polly off.

Polly lost her grip.

"Scrum!" yelled Polly. "I'm falling!"

Scrum was so focused on regaining the point position that he didn't hear her call for help.

It was when he did retake the lead that he looked over his shoulder and saw Polly wasn't on Quill's back anymore. He looked down. She was falling quickly, her arms and legs scrambling to grab the air.

Scrum did a nose dive, but Polly had too much of a lead on him, and she was heading straight for the reflecting pool. He did not think he could catch her.

As Polly shot past the clinic's rooftop, Scrum knew it was too late. He would not be able to reach her before she entered the portal and triggered the implosion.

"Tee-lee-lee! Outside is the best side!" said Quill as she rocketed past Scrum and caught Polly on her back just before she hit the surface of the reflecting pool.

Polly locked her arms around the dragon's neck and dug her thighs into her sides. "Quill, catch Scrum's tail!"

she said, her chest heaving as she tried to catch her breath.

"Scrum-fun!" said Quill, following Scrum back up into the air.

Scrum circled the rooftop once and then dove.

Polly hung on to Quill and hoped the little dragon would be calm in the portal, or at the very least, keep playing the catch-Scrum's-tail game.

Polly had a split-second to examine her reflection before they dove through the glassy surface of reflecting pool. Before she could think about whether or not she looked any different, she saw the building implode. Fire, smoke and debris were following them into the portal.

"Faster!" she screamed.

The dragons beat their wings as hard as they could to stay ahead of the flames and concrete boulders.

When they shot into the familiar landing bay at Guild headquarters, the fire behind them was no more than a steady stream of smoke. On the ground, on either side of the portal, a dozen writers with piles of stone and buckets of mortar stood by to seal the passage.

Polly slid off Quill's back with only one task on her mind.

She didn't stop or talk to anyone until she reached her writing table in the great hall.

Her papers were just as she had left them, held down by the weight of Yulleg's pendant. Polly sat down, put the wooden dragon around her neck, and picked up her pencil. She stifled a groan when she tried to grasp the pencil in her right hand. A few of the writers had watched her come in, their faces strained. Polly glared at them, then turned her attention back to her own private corner of the Guild.

Polly read the first four paragraphs of her vamper-wolf manuscript. Without changing another word or fixing another punctuation mark, she continued writing the fifth paragraph and didn't stop once—except to try writing with her left hand when her right hand got too sore. As imperfect and as messy as the story was, Polly wrote and wrote and wrote until she got to the final scene. She was crying by then—sniffling, bawling, and spewing fat tears down her pale cheeks.

After she had written the final word, Polly put the pencil down and held her right hand with her left, trying to ease the pain. She thought about the small lump of clay in the red plastic egg Ms. Whitford had promised to give to her when she finished her first draft. She just couldn't believe Ms. Whitford was gone. Polly ached to see her dad and to go home. But she was too exhausted to do either, so she crossed her arms on the table, put her head down, and fell dead asleep.

★

Without opening her eyes Polly knew who was singing. It was Quill, and she was stringing together random notes and rhymes in a deep, but somehow light, comforting melody.

"Your father says he needs to see you right away," said Scrum, nudging Polly's head with his snout.

"Okay, okay. I was just a little tired," said Polly, lifting her head. A pencil was stuck to her sweaty cheek.

Quill stopped singing and giggled. "Can I try?" she asked.

Polly held out the white "Scrum Food" pencil.

Quill stuck out her pink tongue and swallowed it instantly. "Yummy in my tummy! Me want more!"

"Come on, you two," said Polly, picking up her vamperwolf story with her left hand. "Where is my dad anyway?"

"He's with the Masterteller," said Scrum.

Her heart sank even further. She didn't want to meet a new masterteller. She wanted Ms. Whitford back.

The dragons stopped at a door just outside the great hall's main entrance. There was an iron door knocker at eye-height. Polly lifted it up and let it drop three times. "You two stay here, and don't get into trouble."

Scrum and Quill smiled cheekily at her. "We won't," they sang in unison.

"Come in, Polly," said her dad, opening the door. He had a solemn air about him.

Polly wrapped her arms around her dad and hugged him.

When he pulled her off, he accidentally banged her broken finger.

Polly whimpered.

"Let's take a look at your finger," said Ms. Whitford. "Come in, sit down, and have some tea with us. We'll get you fixed up.

Shocked, Polly sat down and accepted a tea cup and an icepack from Ms. Whitford, who looked perfectly fine except for slightly singed hair and eyebrows. "Thank you," she mumbled.

The room was similar to Ms. Whitford's writing room at her townhouse except there were no windows to break up the continuous bookshelves, and the furniture was more old-fashioned and worn.

"Is that your lump of clay?" asked Ms. Whitford.

Polly nodded and bit her lip. As she handed the manuscript over, fear was quickly replacing the relief she felt at seeing Ms. Whitford alive.

"I hope I will have time to read this very soon," she said taking it from Polly, glancing through it, and handing it back to her.

"You're alive," said Polly.

"Ted, why don't you bring Polly up to speed."

"We may have destroyed Miriam's clinic too soon," said Polly's dad. "She is still unconscious, and we haven't figured out how to use this thing yet." He held out the metal pendant.

"Were you able to find out anything about it after your father left?" asked Ms. Whitford. "Anything at all?"

"No," said Polly. "Wait! One of the girls, my friend, Natasha, she wants to be a writer too. She told me none of the girls in the clinic ever saw their dragons. But they could see Scrum, so they must be writers."

"Ted, do you think Miriam implanted those dragons as soon as they popped out?"

Polly's dad nodded. "And she's using them to implant other emergent dragons, but how do we stop them?"

"Quill," said Polly, standing up. "Maybe she knows something."

"We have already asked her," sighed Ted, refusing the cup of tea Ms. Whitford offered him. "But she seems... vacant. I can't tell if it's an act, or if she's just naturally obtuse. It's hard to get anything sensible out of her."

Polly sat down. She nodded in agreement even though she believed she might be able to get through to Quill. Before she spoke her thoughts, she noticed a golden urn sitting on a bookshelf. "Is Felix okay too?"

"Tragically, no," said Ms. Whitford. "But everything is as it should be."

Polly sipped her tea. "I'm really glad you're okay," she said awkwardly.

Ms. Whitford sighed. "Overly complex plot lines are easier to resolve in fiction than they are in reality. You cut this, revise that, and no one gets hurt. Reality is just not the same. So many lost dragons. So many lost stories. If Miriam doesn't regain consciousness, the Guild is going to be spending the next decade hunting and training rogue dragons. None of us will have time to write."

There was a knock on the door.

"Yes," said Ms. Whitford.

A writer entered. She was pale.

"Speak," said Ms. Whitford, putting her tea cup down on the tray.

"Miriam Mammozarack just passed away."

Polly shot an angry look at her dad. It was his fault. She got up and walked out of the room.

"Polly! Come back here," shouted Ted.

Polly already knew Quill was gone. "Where is she, Scrum?"

Scrum lay on the ground with his huge head sagging heavily into the stone floor. He snuffled the pile of pale pink dust that was Quill's remains. "I was trying to tell her the story about the first time I went outside with Ms. Whitford, the day we rescued you from the clinic. But she kept interrupting me. She kept saying she wanted to have a big dragon party with lots of pencils to eat and some sky games and that she knew how to call all the dragons in the world to come to the party. I kept telling her to be quiet and listen to my story."

"How? How was she going call all the dragons?"

"She said she knew a special song, and then she started singing. Part way through the song, she burst into flame and turned to ashes." Scrum sniffed.

"Can you sing Quill's song?"

Scrum nodded and sniffed again. "I recognize the tune. But not now. I'm too sad." He curled himself up into a ball on the floor and buried his head and tail in his coils.

Polly ran back to see Ms. Whitford and her dad. "Quill is dead."

"We know," said Ms. Whitford. "Even though Miriam couldn't train her dragon, they were still bonded enough that Quill could not survive her death. Maybe all the dragons she implanted will be gone as well, or worse, they could all end up disfigured and damaged like Felix."

"I don't think so," said Ted, forcefully. "Felix's scars are from surviving the death of his true writer. Those dragons all have living writers out there who they are naturally bonded to. Even though the bond may have been weakened by the implant, I don't think Miriam's death has hurt them. They are probably more lost and confused than anything. The real problem is going to be calling them home. We don't know how Miriam's pendant works."

Polly broke in, speaking quickly. "Scrum said Quill wanted to bring all the dragons home for a big party with a song. Scrum says he can sing the song."

Ms. Whitford stood up. "Finally! I can see the resolution!" She came over and kissed Polly's forehead. "I knew you were the hero of our story, Polly!" With a wide grin splitting her round face, Ms. Whitford turned

Laura Michelle Thomas

to Polly's dad. "Ted, we need every available writer and dragon in the great hall. Polly, get Scrum and meet us there. We're going to have a party, a big dragon party for Quill! I only hope Gratidia will come. We need her."

"She'll come to you, Patti. She always does when you have a true need," said Polly's dad.

"Nevertheless, I am sure she is aware of what is happening, and she could have stopped it on her own by now. Perhaps she believes the situation is good for young dragons. Perhaps I erred in giving her so much freedom."

"Who are you talking about?" asked Polly.

"My dragon," said Ms. Whitford. "Our bond is so strong and so deep that I let her roam freely. She comes and goes as she pleases. I cannot command her. I can only ask her to help us and hope she will."

★

It had taken Polly far too long to rouse Scrum from his weeping coil and get him to come with her to the great hall. They were among the last to arrive and had no choice but to stand at the back of the room, making it extremely difficult for Polly to hear what was going on at the front. She could, however, see the world map on the giant screens. All but a thin rim of lights remained on the furthest edges of the map, and they were still going out every few seconds.

Ms. Whitford climbed up on the round, stone table and held her hands out for silence. "Things are bleak my fellow writers and dragons, but Miriam Mammozarack's dragon—Quill—has given us a departing gift. It is a song, a song that will call these rogue dragons back home, where they can be rehabilitated and, with your help, reunited with their writers."

The crowd murmured its approval.

"Polly! Please bring Scrum forward."

Everyone stepped aside as Polly and Scrum walked solemnly toward the table. Polly looked up at their hopeful, determined faces, unable to make eye contact with anyone because she secretly worried Quill's song was nonsense and might not work.

When they reached the stone table, Polly stood aside while Scrum slid up. Ms. Whitford gestured for Polly to follow him. Wincing, she hoisted herself up and went to stand beside Scrum. The room was filled with dragons and writers, and every eye was on them.

Ms. Whitford called Scrum over. She scratched him under the chin as she whispered to him. Scrum opened his pink mouth and began to sing. Polly did not understand the words, but she was able to follow the bright but guttural tune.

"Everyone join in please," said Ms. Whitford.

Soon the hall was so full of sound, the table began to vibrate ever so slightly beneath Polly's feet.

They sang for a long time.

When Ms. Whitford raised her hands for silence, the room went instantly quiet. Everyone stared up at the map hoping no more lights would go out. For a moment none did, and then one, two, three, four, five, six more lights winked out.

Quill's song had not brought the dragons home. Ms. Whitford closed her eyes and bowed her head in defeat.

At the back of the hall, where Polly and Scrum had been standing, there was a commotion followed by the entrance of a massive white dragon Polly had not seen before. Everyone backed away as she walked up to the table. As she climbed up, the ancient stone cracked but held strong beneath her.

Ms. Whitford had tears running down her cheeks as she opened her arms to Gratidia and swung herself up onto her back. "Again!" she cried. "Sing!"

All voices were raised in unison, filling the hall with vibrations as they had before. But then Gratidia, the matriarch of Scrum's line, joined the chant at a pitch far lower than the rest of the voices. The sound swelled and rattled their bones to the point where Polly could not stand the pain in her finger for another instant.

She was about to stop singing and cry out when Ms. Whitford once again raised her hands for quiet. The voices stopped, but the vibrations continued. Every inch of Guild headquarters was rumbling. The dragons had heard the song and were coming home.

All eyes turned to the screens. There were very few lights left, but not a single one went out.

"To the landing bay!" shouted Ms. Whitford. "We have a lot of work to do!" She looked down from her dragon to where Polly was standing beside Scrum. "It's time for you and Scrum to go home, Polly."

"My story can wait, can't it?" said Polly, looking up with wonder at Ms. Whitford's dragon. "I want to help. There is so much to do, and you need me."

"Look at those screens." Ms. Whitford pointed. "It's going to take years to reunite all those dragons with their writers. Until then, there is going to be a severe shortage of stories. You must write as many stories as you can to help fill the void. The world needs your voice. Don't hold back, not a sentence, not a word. We must finish your training on the writing process as soon as possible so you can polish this story, send it to a publisher, and get on with your next one and your next one and your next one. You must go home now and write. We are counting on you, the whole world is."

"But—I want to stay here and work with you and my Dad."

"Polly, now this nonsense is over, we can all go back to doing what we were meant to do. I was meant to teach you how to train your dragon so you can transform from a wannabe writer into a real, working writer. And I will make time for you. I promise. You will come see me at my townhouse right after you get home. We will pick up where we left off. Now, go!"

Polly turned to go, then stopped. "What about *Dragon by a Tale*?"

"We still don't have a copy of the book," said Ms. Whitford, sliding off Gratidia's back. "And now that Miriam, Felix, and Quill are gone, and Yulleg, too, we aren't going to worry about it. The Guild's secrets are safe. Perhaps someday, Quill's story will be told, but not today."

"Poor Quill," said Polly. "I want to read the story as Yulleg wrote it. He has the silver flash drive. I saw it."

Ms. Whitford feigned a frown. "You went to Stockholm without my permission?"

Polly shrugged. "Yes...um...sorry about that."

Ms. Whitford broke into a grin. "As my predecessor once said, 'all's well that ends well.' Now, it's time, Polly, time to go home."

Polly reached out and stroked the muzzle of the ancient dragon. "How old is she?"

"Oh, Polly! Look how swollen you hand is!" Ms. Whitford sighed. "You are tougher than you look, and that toughness will serve you well in your career as a writer. I'll tell you all about Gratidia another time."

"Do you think Yulleg will ever come back?" ventured Polly.

Ms. Whitford put her arm around Polly's shoulders. "Forget about Yulleg Snoblivski; it's Polly's turn to shine."

Laura Michelle Thomas

CHAPTER TWENTY-ONE

Home

Polly looked down on the very ordinary rooftop of her apartment building. "How do you feel about a trip to Sweden?" she asked Scrum as they circled high above it. It was a beautiful afternoon, and the wind and sun on her cheeks felt sublime.

"The Masterteller said you need to finish your story."

"I know," sighed Polly.

"And do you know what the best part is?"

"I become a rich and famous author?"

Scrum looked at her with uncharacteristic seriousness. "The best part is I get to help you now."

"I'd rather go find Yulleg. I'm dying to read that book. Don't you want to know Quill's story?"

"Of course, but how is a futile search for Yulleg Snoblivski going to help fill the world with stories? And where would the world be without a multitude of tales told from every unique perspective? You need to get writing, young lady."

Polly smiled. "Listen to you! When did you get all wise and start talking like Ms. Whitford?"

"When I found out her dragon is my grandmother."

"Who told you that?"

"The great and wise Gratidia told me so herself. While you were saying your goodbyes, she told me I am descended from a long line of famous literary dragons, and that I have a great duty to perform."

"Really? What duty?"

"Helping you turn your lumps of clay into masterpieces."

Polly thought about the idea of creating masterpieces of literature that would be read generation after generation like the works of the great writers. It sounded pretty good. "Let's go home," she said.

Scrum arched his back and puffed out his scrawny chest as he wafted down to the sidewalk in front of the building.

When Polly buzzed, her mom answered and was absolutely thrilled her daughter was home. When the elevator doors opened, she was waiting for Polly with open arms and a huge smile on her face. Mother and daughter walked down the hall with their arms wrapped tightly around each other. All the while Polly's mom fussed about Polly's broken finger.

"I'm fine, Mom. It doesn't even hurt anymore," said Polly as they went inside. "I'm only home for a few minutes. Ms. Whitford is anxious for me to finish my story."

"Of course, Polly, but let me fix you a quick snack before you go."

"I'm not hungry," said Polly, following her into the kitchen. "Mom?"

"What is it?"

"Do you think Dad will...do you think he'll ever move back home?"

Polly's mom clapped her hands together with delight. "Absolutely, not!" she said. "We have a better plan for all of us."

"We? What plan?" groaned Polly. She braced herself for another round of roast beef dinners.

Polly's mom looked up from the cutting board where she was making up a plate of cheese, cold cuts, and crackers. "Your dad and I have decided you will stay with me during the week and stay with him every weekend. He is working for a new tractor farming guild or some such thing and will not be traveling any more. So he says."

Polly blinked. Was she hearing her mom right? Weekends at Guild headquarters? She looked at Scrum, who was waiting patiently for her in the hallway, and smiled.

"Well, Polly, what do you think? He seems convinced you will love it. Apparently, his new apartment is just your style."

Polly just about started bouncing up and down like Quill. She hugged her mom. "But I'll miss you."

"Oh, for goodness sake! We'll see each other all week. I'm really pleased you and your dad are going to be spending time together. And, if you have something going on here with your friends or Ms. Whitford on a weekend, you can just stay home with me. This is meant to be good for you Polly, but we don't want to force you."

"It's a good idea, Mom. Thank you. Thank you. Thank you!" Polly put a slice of salami and cheese on a cracker and took a bite.

"I told you everything would work out for the best, and I believe it has," said Polly's mom as she helped herself to a piece of cheese. "That reminds me—I have another surprise. Follow me."

Polly followed her mom to her bedroom. "Your father's tractor guild or whatever it is told me you won a writing challenge while you were at the clinic, and the prize was a bedroom makeover fit for a Nobel Prize-winning author."

Polly walked into her room with Scrum on her heels. "Oh, Mom! It's amazing!"

Polly stood in a replica of Dr. Mammozarack's bedroom complete with wall-to-wall bookshelves and the gorgeous four-poster bed with the indigo silk bedding. Polly went over to the shelves, which were loaded with books: all the classic novels, bestselling contemporary novels, books on how to write novels, plays, essays, and poems. There were three shelves of books, that a carefully left note addressed to Polly explained were written by her dad under his many pseudonyms. Yulleg's complete collection was there too. There were antique books and books hot off the presses and an entire shelf loaded with blank journals.

"It's perfect," she said.

"I thought it might be a bit too lavish for you, but your father insisted he knew better." Polly's mom look mystified for a moment. "What a change. After being gone so much while you were growing up, it amazes me that he seems to know you better than I do. Anyway, I am sorry to say, though, Polly, that your grandmother's antique mirror went missing during the renovation. You know the one I mean: the one with the white, wooden frame with the swirls in it. Right?"

Polly smiled at Scrum as she nodded. "Of course. That's too bad, but I think this room makes up for losing one old mirror."

"Wait here one second," said her Mom, leaving the room. "I have one more thing to give you before you go see Ms. Whitford."

Scrum came over and put his head on Polly's shoulder. She reached up and scratched his hairy chin.

"It feels strange to be back in this room," said Polly. "But I absolutely love it."

"Me too," said Scrum.

"Do you think you can keep from smashing it to bits?"

"I can try. Just don't get me too excited."

Polly's mom burst into the bedroom with a wrapped gift. "Here you go."

Polly accepted the gift and walked over to the bed. She put the gift down and unwrapped it quickly. It was a new laptop.

Polly looked at Scrum.

Scrum stared at the laptop and started drooling.

Laura Michelle Thomas

Polly's mom sniffed. "You know, I thought we got rid of that smell when we renovated, but it seems to be back. How strange. I'll have to talk to the contractor."

Polly suppressed a giggle. "I love my new laptop. Thanks, Mom. I can't wait to set it up, but I have to go. Ms. Whitford will be waiting for me."

"Of course. Off you go. Dinner will be ready when you get home."

Polly put her new laptop in a backpack and slipped the bag over her shoulders.

"Your bike is in the storage locker, Polly. Do you want me to get it out for you?"

Polly looked at Scrum. "That's okay, Mom. I'll walk."

When they were outside, Polly took the laptop out of her backpack and held it out. "Do you want it?"

Scrum licked his lips hungrily. "Yes...ah...no...yes... no! No! Thank you, no! And I mean it—thank you, but no!"

"Really?"

"I promised my grandmother I would do my duty, and I will."

Without saying a word, Polly put the laptop away, put the backpack on, and climbed on Scrum's back.

Moments later, Polly and Scrum stood on the doorstep of Ms. Whitford's townhouse. The glossy green door looked exactly the same as it had the first day she had come there, panicked because she had woken up with an albino dragon in her bedroom. She stood on the welcome mat gathering her thoughts. She put an arm around Scrum's neck and lifted the dragon door knocker. It was a warm afternoon, and beads of sweat bubbled up through the pale surface of her skin. She peeked through the window and watched Ms. Whitford's shadowy outline get bigger as she approached the door.

Ms. Whitford smiled. "Welcome back."

Polly smiled. Ms. Whitford was wearing a white knit tam just like the one Polly had worn that day at the school library. "I love your hat."

"Come in! Please! Both of you."

Moments later, Polly's shoes were off and neatly tucked away in the shoe rack in the entryway, and she was sitting on the slightly tattered, denim-upholstered easy chair in Ms. Whitford's bright and airy writing room. The desk was tidy and had changed little since her last visit. There was still a neat stack of books, a jar filled with uniform HB pencils all with their eraser ends up, an open notebook, a computer, a printer, and Ms. Whitford's leather-bound manuscript.

"You still want to be my third reviewer, don't you?"

"Very much," said Polly scratching Scrum's head. He was coiled up beside her on a thick rug, his eyelids drooping heavily over his pink eyes.

"Well, this is exciting because now you get to see what Scrum can do for you. Let's get to sculpting your story, and perhaps at the end of today's lesson you'll be ready to take this home with you." She tapped the leather bound manuscript.

"Thank you for my new bedroom," said Polly.

"It's our pleasure, Polly. And have you agreed to spend weekends with us?"

"Us?"

Ms. Whitford nodded. "Here, have a cinnamon bun. I've missed these terribly."

"What do you mean us?" asked Polly.

"It's not what you're thinking. I mean 'us' as in the Guild. Spending weekends at headquarters will expedite your training and allow you to take the oath sooner, perhaps, than would otherwise be possible. You need to have at least a dozen pieces of writing published before we can induct you as a full member. Spending more time surrounded by other writers will give you the support you need to achieve that level of success. None of us did it alone. Won't you have a cinnamon bun?"

Polly shook her head. "Just tea please. I don't want my fingers to get sticky."

"Okay, then," said Ms. Whitford, "please take your place at my desk, and let's warm up." She put a blank sheet of paper and a slippery pen out for Polly. She took one of the pencils out of the container and tossed it at Scrum, who caught it with his tongue and started sucking on it as he closed his eyes. She opened up the deep drawer and took out the three-minute timer and the red plastic egg.

Polly took the manuscript out of her backpack and gave it to Ms. Whitford, who, in turn, handed her the egg. Polly took out the clay and squished it in her good hand. She liked the feeling of it oozing through her fingers.

"Sit down," said Ms. Whitford as she moved over to the easy chair. "You are going to write without thinking, twice, for three minutes, while I read through this and see what kind of clay we have to work with. I assume you can write with that splint on."

Polly nodded.

"Good." said Ms. Whitford.

Polly wrote for three minutes without stopping or even pausing and did it again on the other side of the paper. When she was done she looked over at Ms. Whitford, who was still reading her story.

"Did the focusing worksheet help?" she asked without looking up.

"Yes. It was very helpful."

"I would agree. This is a clever piece of writing: 'How I Became a Vamperwolf.' It needs a fair bit of trimming and rearranging—substantial revisions—but it's an entertaining story and deserves some time and effort."

Polly was immensely relieved.

"Scrum. Wake up!" said Ms. Whitford swatting the dragon on the head with Polly's manuscript.

Scrum opened his eyes and sprang to attention.

"I would like you to read this story and give me feedback on the big stuff like plot, point of view, settings, and characters. Do you understand? Big stuff only. I don't care about spelling mistakes or a misplaced comma or word. Just the big stuff. Anything that breaks the story's spell."

"Yes, Masterteller," said Scrum.

Ms. Whitford put the manuscript on the floor in front of him, and Scrum started reading.

"While he is doing his job, I think you and I can have a cinnamon bun and a cup of tea."

"Okay," said Polly, watching Scrum nervously. "What do I do next?"

"Well. You have accomplished something many wannabe writers simply cannot—write a complete first draft with a beginning, middle, and end. Many aspiring writers are completely waylaid by their dragons before they write the last scene. They get lost doing endless revisions of the introduction. I mean think about it, Polly. How can you possibly evaluate the beginning of your story when you haven't even written the end? That's pure dragon logic—to nitpick every minor detail when you're supposed to be having fun and exploring the limits of your creativity." Ms. Whitford paused to take a sip of tea.

"Good for you for making a lump of clay, Polly. But now we are moving into an entirely different stage of the writing process—the editing or revision stage—and you may end up here for a while as you sculpt your lump of clay with ever-more refined tools. You have written your first draft, but it may take four or five rounds of revisions to get your story as good as you can make it."

"Oh," said Polly, feeling more anxious about the coming criticism from Scrum.

"We are going to start by revising the major elements of your story—plot, point of view, characters, settings. Next time, we will ask Scrum to review your second draft and give you feedback on these big changes. Once he is happy with those, we will ask him to look at your writing style and tone and evaluate little things like diction, your use of figurative devices, places where you tell rather than show. Anything that is confusing or makes the story fuzzy in your reader's imagination will have to be revised. With each pass through your story, you will refine your edits. From rewriting scenes and cutting characters and settings, you will work your way down to cutting excess words like said, that, very, rather, little, pretty, fancy words, and awkward adverbs. You will keep refining your draft until we all love it, and it's as good as you can make it at this point in your career."

"How many drafts will I have to do?"

"Maybe three, maybe twenty."

Polly groaned. "Will it be ready to send to a publisher then? I'm really excited about that step."

Ms. Whitford handed Polly a napkin so she could wipe some frosting off her nose. "Oh, no, not a chance."

"When will I be able to send it?"

"Once you and Scrum agree your draft is as good as you can make it, it still needs to be proofread line by line, word by word. Scrum is going to be exceptional at that. Then, and only then, will we start looking for a publisher."

"Then can I send it in?"

Ms. Whitford shook her head.

"What? Why not?"

"Once we find a suitable publisher—one who already deals in your genre and subject matter—you will have to format your manuscript exactly as a publisher specifies with whatever other documents or information they want to see. In the case of a novel, that might be the first three chapters and a synopsis plus an author biography. With a short story, usually a simple, snappy cover letter is all they want, along with the entire manuscript."

"What if I send it to a contest instead?"

"You still have to follow the format the contest organizer is asking for, otherwise you will have zero chance of winning. If you don't care enough to respect their rules, they have every right to put your story in the shredder. It's that simple. Not following the rules or submission guidelines will kill your chances before they even read one word. This is a highly competitive business, but if you take it seriously and respect the industry, you will make it."

Polly looked glumly at Scrum. She had been so happy with her first draft, she thought maybe she only had to proofread it once and send it in.

"I'm done," said Scrum, looking up from the last page of Polly's manuscript.

Ms. Whitford looked very pleased. "Excellent, Scrum. Let's hear your recommendations. I want you to look directly at Polly and tell her—with love and respect— what changes you would like her to make for draft number two." Ms. Whitford addressed Polly. "I want you to look at Scrum—with love and respect—and listen to what he tells you."

"Do you both understand?"

"I think so," said Polly.

"Yes," said Scrum.

"You may begin," said Ms. Whitford.

Scrum cleared his throat. "Polly...the introduction is too long. You can show me the main character instead of telling me a bunch of things about her background that don't really matter to the story."

He paused.

Polly nodded. It was hard to hear Scrum's criticisms but also fascinating.

"Things are too easy for your protagonist. They should get harder and harder because some force is trying to stop her. Your climax needs to be more tense."

"Good, Scrum," said Ms. Whitford.

"And one more plot thing," he said.

"Yes?" said Ms. Whitford.

"The ending needs to connect back to the beginning."

"Good. What about point of view?" asked Ms. Whitford.

"Actually," said Scrum looking at Ms. Whitford, tentatively. "I like the first person point of view for this story. It goes with the title and theme. It makes a lot of sense and helps the unity of the story."

Polly was elated.

"As for settings...she has too many," he continued.

"Tell Polly, not me," said Ms. Whitford.

Laura Michelle Thomas

Scrum looked back at Polly. "You only have two thousand words and too many settings. I would cut half of them."

"And what about characters, Scrum? How do you think she did?"

"She doesn't have too many—I mean, Polly, you don't have too many, but you waste a lot of words describing what they look like. I don't care what colour their hair is. I just want to know the stuff about them that matters for the story, just details that make the story more interesting and meaningful."

Polly was almost having an out-of-body experience as she listened to Scrum. She hated him for ripping apart her story, but, on the other hand, she was happy to be receiving such clear, concrete, specific things to fix. She was starting to think of ways she could really improve her story and starting to feel more confident it could be good enough to win a prize or get published. A feeling of excitement about the writing process and working with Scrum bubbled up inside her. "Is there anything else?" she asked.

"You could make the antagonist meaner," offered Scrum.

"Excellent work you two," said Ms. Whitford, clapping her hands together. "Polly I'd like you to bring me draft number two tomorrow with all those changes." She stood up and opened her arms wide.

Polly got up and gave her a hug.

"You're not going to be a wannabe writer much longer, Polly. Well done. Scrum, you too. You will make your grandmother very proud indeed."

"Thank you for everything," said Polly. "Thank you too, Scrum."

Scrum bowed low before Ms. Whitford and Polly.

"Now," said the Masterteller. "I am going to cut today's session short so I can get back to headquarters. You cannot imagine how difficult it is to reunite dragons with their writers. But before I go, Polly, I would like to officially hire you as one of my reviewers for this book—the first book of mine that will be published with my name on the front cover. As I told you during my visit to your school, I have been a ghostwriter my whole career. But I think that is going to change now. You've inspired me to spend less time writing other people's stories and more time writing my own." She took the leather-bound manuscript off her desk and handed it to Polly. "I hope this story inspires you in return."

Polly hugged the thick manuscript to her chest. "Thank you, Ms. Whitford."

"Now, don't put reading this ahead of working on the second draft of your story, okay?"

Polly nodded. "I promise."

"I don't even want you to open it until you have finished your second draft."

"I won't," said Polly.

A huge white dragon appeared outside in the backyard. Ms. Whitford smiled at Polly. "Off you go then. Your second draft isn't going to write itself. No time for visiting with Grandma now, Scrum. On the weekend, maybe."

Ms. Whitford ushered Polly and Scrum out the front door and waved goodbye. Polly held the bound manuscript in both hands as she walked down the driveway. Then she stopped and looked back over her shoulder to make sure the glossy green front door was shut. With tremulous hands she undid the leather laces holding the leather cover closed.

"What are you doing?" said Scrum, when he noticed Polly wasn't climbing on his back.

"Sh!" said Polly as she unwound the laces. "I just want to see what the title is." Polly slowly opened the leather cover and saw the crisp white title page.

"Hurry up!" said Scrum impatiently. He nudged Polly with a shoulder. "That new laptop of yours made me hungry."

"*Polly Wants to Be a Writer*," she read aloud, "by Patience Whitford."

"I know Polly wants to be a writer," said Scrum only halfway paying attention. His stomach rumbled, and he belched loudly. "That's not news. The question is: Will her dragon starve to death before she becomes one?"

"No, Scrum. Look." She thrust the manuscript in front of Scrum's plate-sized nostrils.

"That's the title of Ms. Whitford's book—*Polly Wants to be a Writer.*"

Scrum looked at Polly and smiled. "My grandma was right. We're going to be famous."

Polly grinned as she wrapped up the manuscript back in its leather binding and put it in her backpack along with her new laptop, the red plastic egg with the clay inside, and her vamperwolf manuscript. She climbed on Scrum's back and touched the dragon pendant around her neck. She was eager to work on her second draft and to spend her first weekend at the Guild with her dad and Ms. Whitford. Maybe she could help them find Natasha's dragon.

"Fly, Scrum!" she said.

Scrum used Ms. Whitford's driveway like a trampoline to launch the two of them into the warm spring sky.

Polly promised herself she wouldn't read Ms. Whitford's novel until her second draft was done, and it was a promise she kept.

A WRITING CHALLENGE FOR YOU

On pages 152 and 153, Polly completes a focusing worksheet for her vamperwolf story. My challenge to you is to use the details on Polly's worksheet to write a short story of no more than two thousand words of your own. Use Polly's title and all the information provided to build your story. Follow the six-step writing process outlined below, just like Polly did, and then send me your story. I will consider it for publication on my website. If it's not quite ready for publication, I will read it and send you some feedback to help you get it there.

Use this exercise as an opportunity to train your literary dragon—that nasty, yet intelligent, voice inside you that critiques your work almost as soon as an idea floats across your imagination. Use this exercise to figure out how and when to use your dragon as you go step by step through the writing process. Have fun, and don't be shy about emailing me or posting a question or comment on my website if you get muddled. After all, where would Polly be without her Ms. Whitford?

The Six-Step Writing Process & When To Use Your Dragon

Step 1: Write Into Your Idea – No Dragons Allowed

Get an idea and write freely about it. When I wrote this book, I started with an idea, and I just sat down and started writing until I could start to visualize the main characters. I said yes to everything that popped into my imagination, no matter how silly it seemed at the time. This can be such a fun step. There are no boundaries except those your inner dragon creates. Tell him to be quiet so that you can work. Send him to stay with Grandma Gratidia for a while. Whatever it takes, be dragon free and write a lot.

Step 2: Do Some Research — No Dragons Allowed

Do some research to develop different elements of your story. Use your own experiences, use the experiences of others. Write freely. For this book, I pulled from the short story writing course I have been teaching for several years. I used the course material and my memories of interacting with young writers to draft an outline for the story and create Polly and Ms. Whitford.

Ms. Whitford had Polly write paragraphs about her plot, protagonist, and primary setting. She also had Polly visualize and write about her main scenes: the opening, climax, and ending. There is no right way to do research. You can go inside yourself or to the outside world through online searches, traveling, or talking to people who have had the kind of experience you are writing about.

As in the first step, keep your dragon quiet. Say yes to everything and keep writing.

Step 3: Make Some Choices (Focus) — No Dragons Allowed

At this point, you need to realize you cannot put the world into a single story. You need to decide what your story is really going to be about. A useful trick for helping you focus your story idea is to create a working title and a theme statement. Both of these may change as you go deeper into your story, but putting them front and centre early on will help you stay on track.

My theme statement for this book was and still is: writers are made not born and most wannabe writers don't understand that. My working title for this book was *The Junior Authors Guide to Writing and Getting Published*, but that changed. In the end, the working title became the subtitle, but along the way it helped me remember my reason for writing this story.

Step 4: Create Your Lump of Clay – No Dragons Allowed

Once you have written into your idea, done some research into your story world, and decided on a working title and theme statement, it's time to write your first draft. I cannot stress enough how important it is that you keep your dragon locked up during this step. If you don't, he will be in your face telling you your work is not good enough. Realize, please, that a first draft is never good enough for an audience, and that's okay. It's supposed to be a lump of clay (a complete lump of clay) but nothing more.

For this book, I just wrote without stopping. I said yes to every setting, every character, every plot twist, no matter how complicated or tangential. Do you remember that scene in the landing bay where Ms. Whitford spins around and divines the location of the silver flash drive? That was originally written with an old woman, Ms. Whitford's mother, who I imagined as a wise woman and healer. The old woman got cut on the second draft, but I transferred her powers and some of her dialogue to Ms. Whitford.

It's nuggets like this that come out of you when you let yourself have fun with the first draft, making sure there are no inner dragons in the room. If you let your dragon interfere before your first draft is done, your creativity will be stifled, and you might end up hating creative writing because, like Polly, you will not be able to write all the way to the last scene.

Do not restrict yourself at this stage in the process. Be free. Explore your soul. Comment on the world. Go wild, but make sure you don't stop until you write an ending. Until you have a complete lump of clay, you cannot not go on to the next step. When your lump is finished, it's time to turn your dragon loose.

Laura Michelle Thomas

Step 5: Sculpt Your Lump of Clay – It's Dragon Time!

Now it's time for your inner critic to shine. You are going to go through your manuscript several times from beginning to end. With each pass, with each round of revisions, you will be focusing on ever-smaller elements of your story. Start by fixing the major elements first: character, plot, and setting. With each pass, get more refined in your revisions. Cut away the excess words and scenes. Revise. Rewrite, until you are happy with all the elements and your story is unified. Pass it through the sieve Ms. Whitford talked to Polly about. If nothing gets filtered out, your story is unified. Unity in a story means that every element (theme, title, plot, characters, settings, tone, etc.) is singing the same song in the same way, and that your story is told in as few words as possible. This could take several drafts. Finalize your title during this step too.

To give you an idea of how much work this step in the writing process can be, let me share how this novel went during the revision stage. My first draft was 71,059 words. Then I cut everything that didn't serve the plot and theme. My second draft was a slim 57,791 words. My third draft, in which I had to tidy up some plot inconstancies, was thinned down even further to 54, 611 words. My fourth draft, in which I thickened up my descriptions of character and setting, was back up to 65,570 words. My fifth draft grew again slightly to 66,043 words because I looked for places where I needed to fill in the blanks with a little more detail so you wouldn't have to work too hard. (I actually aim to have my reader not have to work at all. I strive to make the words invisible.)

My dragon and I worked together from big edits to small. It's tough, and there were days I really wanted to give up—days that my dragon told me I suck or that it was too hard to fix something. But, my appreciation and respect for my inner dragon's talent outweighed my fear and exhaustion, so I didn't give up. And, the truth is, I liked Polly's story more and more with each round of editing.

In moments like those, when your dragon has you by the nose, remember this is only one of many stories you will write if you take your passion for writing seriously. When you remember that your life's work and masterpieces are in your future, it's easier to make changes and let things go so you can simplify, strengthen, and deepen the story you are currently working on. The other good news is that the more you write, the faster and more clinical revisions become. But it's never easy. It's not meant to be.

Step 6: Proofread and Format Your Final Draft – Dragons Needed!

Once your manuscript is as good as you can get it, go through it with your dragon's sharpest teeth. Proofread your final draft and clean up all the typos and awkward phrases. Figure out your bad habits like forgetting commas or overusing words like "that" or "very." Then format your manuscript properly for the publisher you are sending it to. Be sure to read the publisher's submission guidelines and follow them perfectly. And, for goodness sake, don't send a vampire story for teens to a company that only sells children's picture books or cookbooks for seniors! And for those of you who are under twenty-two, understand that, as a general rule, big publishers only consider work by adult authors with agents. If you are young and new, submit your work to markets that fit your age and are open to unsolicited manuscripts from un-agented young writers.

Now what?

Once you send off a piece of writing, you must get on to your next piece. Just keep writing. Put in your hours. Practice your craft. Share your work. Do it again a thousand times, and you'll get good, really good.

Professional writers are not born; they are made through thousands of hours of practice mixed with a dash of talent. Every five minutes you spend first-draft writing, editing, proofreading, and formatting adds up. Every imperfect page, every completed lump of clay, gets you one step closer to making your dream come true. Don't let your dragon tell you anything different. If Polly can do it, you can too.

Laura Michelle Thomas, M.A. is a professional writer and story-teller with a passion for helping young writers jump-start their literary careers. Her company, Laura Thomas Communications, fosters the development of young writers worldwide through quality contests, conferences, books, blogs, and educational materials. To find out more please visit:

www.laurathomascommunications.com

Printed in Canada